A Candlelight Ecstasy Romance ®

"YOU WANT ME. ADMIT IT," BRIAN GROWLED. . . .

As he spoke he looked down into her face, his passionate eyes holding her gaze captive, his voice thick with desire. Then slowly, tenderly, his fingers began an exploring path across her forehead and down her cheek. With infinite care he began to slip the top of her dress down from her pale shoulders. The throbbing pleasure of his caresses sent a wave of fire coursing downward through Rowan's body. She could not stop him now; his touch was too thrilling to be denied. And it was all true. She did want him now and somehow nothing else seemed important. All other considerations had suddenly been swept away . . .

BRIAN'S CAPTIVE

Alexis Hill Jordan

A CANDLELIGHT ECSTASY ROMANCE ®

Published by
Dell Publishing Co., Inc.
1 Dag Hammarskjold Plaza
New York, New York 10017

Dell ® TM 681510, Dell Publishing Co., Inc.
Candlelight Ecstasy Romance®, 1,203,540, is a registered
trademark of Dell Publishing Co., Inc.,
New York, New York.

ISBN: 0-440-10425-4

Printed in the United States of America
First printing—August 1983

To my understanding husband

To Our Readers:

We have been delighted with your enthusiastic response to Candlelight Ecstasy Romances®, and we thank you for the interest you have shown in this exciting series.

In the upcoming months we will continue to present the distinctive sensuous love stories you have come to expect only from Ecstasy. We look forward to bringing you many more books from your favorite authors and also the very finest work from new authors of contemporary romantic fiction.

As always, we are striving to present the unique, absorbing love stories that you enjoy most—books that are more than ordinary romance.

Your suggestions and comments are always welcome. Please write to us at the address below.

Sincerely,

The Editors
Candlelight Romances
1 Dag Hammarskjold Plaza
New York, New York 10017

CHAPTER ONE

Rowan Strickland angled her blue Chevette into a parking place between a sleek black Jaguar and a Lincoln Continental.

Wryly she eyed the two posh automobiles, and then swiveled her head to take in the long curved driveway lined with equally flashy transportation. The brick mansion dominating the head of the circular drive belonged to famed Washington hostess April Coster, whose socialite parties had become legendary over the past thirty years. Though Rowan had attended similar high-powered gatherings with her former fiancé, she'd never before been to a Coster extravaganza.

Her boss, Bill Emory, had wangled the invitation—a testimonial to his clout as one of the nation's most respected and feared political columnists. But now that he'd done his part, she had to follow through.

Rowan's stomach knotted as she checked the miniature tape recorder in her beaded handbag again. As the only girl in a family of rambunctious boys, she had learned early to force herself to take dares despite, and sometimes because of, her inner qualms. But the thing she was nerving herself to do now gave her more than the usual misgivings. She was here to get some information from a man who might well be dangerous. Though the gossip columns made him sound like a harmless playboy, Bill had received a tip that linked him with some very questionable international business dealings.

"I just heard something really big!" Bill had shouted when he blew out of his office that afternoon like an avenging tornado. "The Senate Committee on Foreign Trade is about to question Brian Turner, the big honcho at Turner Electronics."

Rowan had glanced up from the file of Securities and Exchange Commission rulings she was summarizing and eyed her boss speculatively. He was a large, bluff-looking man with a shock of white hair and bright blue eyes. But his affable exterior hid a probing mind and the tenacity of a bulldog. His freelance news organization had a formidable reputation in Washington for ferreting out secrets and chicanery in high places and getting them into print before anyone else.

"Turner Electronics," she had asked, "don't they make chips for personal computers and arcade games?" She knew because Turner's latest game had recently been written up in one of the national news magazines. Since she occasionally went with her friends after lunch to the local arcade to try her luck at Asteroids and Space Invaders, she had perused the story with interest. "Some of those games are technologically very sophisticated," she volunteered.

"Don't I know it," Bill growled in agreement. "And Turner's are among the best." He gave her a sharp look from beneath his bushy eyebrows. "But some of his chips may be winding up in the wrong hands."

Rowan's ears had pricked up. "Really?" she exclaimed, watching her boss alertly as he jammed his broad hands into his pockets.

"Yes, they may have been found in military equipment —in countries that aren't exactly our allies."

"You mean Turner is selling to those people?"

"That's what I don't know. He refused point-blank to talk to me. Says he can't make any comment before the Senate hearing." Leaning forward, Bill drummed his fingers impatiently on the desk's surface. "But at least he admitted that there *is* going to be a hearing."

Rowan watched her boss's normally ruddy complexion darken as he began to pace irritably the length of the small office. Turning abruptly back to Rowan, he snapped, "Turner knows the score, and all my instincts tell me that he's covering something up. Damn, I wish Wally was back from his South American trip. He'd get us some hard information that we could go to print with. I guess I'll just have to do it myself."

Rowan recognized the tone of seething excitement in Bill's gravelly voice. It meant that he had sunk his teeth into this thing and wasn't going to let go until he had the whole story. But tension-producing legwork had long since undermined his constitution. He'd already had one heart attack. And that's why he had hired several assistants to be his eyes, ears, and legs.

Rowan had thought she'd jump right into the thick of Washington intrigue when she'd joined his staff a year and a half ago. Unfortunately Bill had an old-fashioned, protective attitude toward women. And the exciting assignments always went to the guys on the staff, while she was chained to her desk with a stack of boring paper work. But now, with Wally Harding, Bill's star reporter, gone, maybe she was being handed a golden opportunity to change things.

Gripping the edge of her desk, she asked as casually as possible, "Why don't you let me have a shot at it? This SEC material can wait, and if I don't find something out, you can go ahead and bring in Wally when he gets back next week."

Bill had looked doubtful. "Listen, Rowan, this is big stuff. It could even be dangerous, and only a very experienced reporter should take it on."

Despite the nervous excitement that almost made her tremble, Rowan regarded her boss steadily. "Come on, Bill," she forced herself to answer. "At least give me a chance. You said you hired me because I was a woman with spunk and creativity. But all you've let me do is push papers around a desk. Give me this assignment. If I muff it, you won't hear another complaint out of me."

Bill had eyed her oval face and crop of fiery curls uncertainly. But then, rubbing a hand against his chin, he conceded, "Well, this *could* be one assignment where you have an advantage over even Wally, our boy wonder."

Rowan couldn't help grinning. Wally, despite his unprepossessing appearance, had a reputation around the capital for pulling off some quite unlikely stunts in the name of investigative reporting. But Bill's next words sobered her expression. "You are a damn good-looking female," he went on, "and Turner has a weakness for the ladies. I happen to know he's going to be at April Coster's big bash for the Children's Fund tonight. If I get you an invite, do you think you could do anything with that?"

Rowan didn't hesitate. "Just what do you have in mind?"

Bill's eyes lit up mischievously. "I think you know what I mean. Can you get into Turner's good graces and pump him for a little information?"

Could she? Rowan willed herself not to let Bill see her mixed reaction. Playing Mata Hari was something she wasn't so confident about. But under the pressure of the moment the decision came quickly.

"OK, you're on," she agreed.

Yet once Bill had left, the long-legged redhead leaned back in her chair and took a deep, steadying breath. Despite her bravado, she felt anything but confident. For the past few months, since she and her fiancé, Charles Fogel, had split up so painfully, she had avoided relationships with men. Just the thought of getting tangled up with an aggressive male made her feel uneasy. But this opportunity was just too important to pass up. And, anyway, she remonstrated, what was she afraid of? She would meet this Turner character at a party, a public place, for heaven's sake! What could happen? The question galvanized her into action. Pushing back her chair and grabbing a notebook, she headed down the hall to the Emory Organization library.

Rowan spent the next two hours in Bill's research files, feverishly trying to learn everything she could about Brian Turner. From dozens of articles in newspapers, magazines, technical journals, and even gossip sheets, she was able to piece together a provocative profile of the man.

An MIT graduate and the scion of a well-to-do Boston family, he had founded his own electronics company very soon after taking his engineering degree. Although his father's money had gone into the project, he had quickly made a startling success in his own right by getting in on the ground floor of the computer game craze. Now, though he was only in his mid-thirties, he was a leader in the field and well on the way to being a multimillionaire.

In light of Bill's suspicions Rowan was surprised to note that Turner's company had supported a whole range of educational programs designed to familiarize high school students with computer technology. Turner had even set up a scholarship fund at his alma mater for disadvantaged youths interested in data processing.

But it was the social side of his life that made her lift an eyebrow. Over the years he had been linked romantically with a whole string of jet set heiresses, models, actresses, and pop singers.

Rowan studied a photograph of his rakish profile, trying to get some hint of the mind that informed it. The man was such a bundle of contradictions. Certainly the media hype spread before her gave no hint of anything sinister in his background. In fact, with his philanthropies and his romantic social life, he sounded like an all-American Prince Charming. But what did the media really know? It would be so easy for those blatant good looks to hide a ruthless character.

Rowan had mulled over the problem all afternoon, alternately feeling confident and then apprehensive about taking him on. Now in the safe haven of her car, she looked down ruefully at the plunging neckline of her new emerald-green jersey dress. The way the soft material clung to her curves had made her feel uncertain in the dressing room at Lord and Taylor that afternoon. But the salesgirl's enthusiasm had been contagious. "If you want to look really sexy, that's the perfect dress!" she exclaimed. And as she studied her reflection Rowan had agreed. But it was one thing to look like a sex goddess in the privacy of a dressing room, and quite another to appear in this guise at a Washington soiree. *Quite a come on,* she told herself. Maybe she had gone too far.

To prolong the moment of truth a bit, she pulled down the sun visor and studied her classic, delicately sculpted features in the mirror. At the beauty shop the hairdresser had coaxed her natural curls into a feathered upsweep. And her blue eyes behind their fringe of thick lashes were emphasized by the careful makeup job she'd done. With her hectic schedule and her preference for a more natural look, she rarely paid so much attention to her makeup. Part of her mind was surprised at the pleasure her polished appearance gave her. Maybe she really did have the makings of a seductress, after all. Tonight would certainly be a good test.

Taking a deep breath, Rowan opened the car door, swung her shapely legs out onto the blacktop, and started resolutely for the mansion at the head of the drive. The stiletto heels of her gilded sandals clicking on April Coster's brick steps were soon drowned out by the sound of a string orchestra and the murmur of scores of cultivated voices. Bright light streamed into the humid July night from the open door and the gallery of Palladian windows along the high portico. Rowan paused just inside the threshold, taking in the crowded scene with interest. She could see into a large drawing room where elegantly clad guests clustered in little knots among the antiques. Tuxedoed waiters circulated among the groups, bearing silver trays of champagne glasses and appealing canapés. The whole scene looked like something out of an elegant stage production. And Rowan suddenly felt as though she were an actress about to assume a role. It was not an unfamiliar sensation, she reflected wryly. Many Washington cocktail parties were like this. You chose your mask for the evening and played your part.

While making her entrance Rowan coolly dismissed the interested male glances that followed her swaying progress across the room. As she moved forward a waiter passed balancing a tray with bubbling glasses of champagne. To give herself something to do with her hands, she reached for one. Taking several small sips, she looked around at the scene, her blue eyes assessing everyone. It was quite an impressive crowd, liberally laced with senators, ambassadors, high administration officials, and the elite of Washington society. Normally she would have sought out her hostess, she thought, spotting the dowager with her silver chignon and beaded blue shantung shift. But since she had never been introduced to April Coster, she decided against it.

It was better to get right to the business at hand. Where was Brian Turner? Rowan wandered in a deliberately casual fashion from the drawing room to the dining room with its delicate oriental wallpaper and pale green hangings, and then out onto the broad flagstone terrace lit with gay paper lanterns. Elegantly dressed partygoers studded the paths of the elaborate garden below, which sloped down to a spectacular overlook of Rock Creek Park. Rowan wove her way among them, heading for the shadows of a holly bower halfway down the gentle incline.

"Quite a layout, isn't it?" an unctuous voice murmured close to her ear. Turning, she encountered the suggestive gaze of a rotund lobbyist she had fended off at several Capitol Hill receptions.

"Well, what's that muckraker you work for up to these

days?" he asked, as his brightly observant eyes wandered over the clinging fabric of her dress.

"You know that would be telling," Rowan parried lightly.

"Not going to give me an advance scoop on the next Washington scandal?" He moved closer, his voice lowering to an insinuating purr.

Under the circumstances it was definitely not a subject Rowan wanted to pursue. Taking a step backwards, she gave him a cool look. Understanding the unspoken message, he returned a well-practiced smile of regret. After a few more moments of idle conversation he excused himself to pursue a more responsive quarry.

And Rowan was glad. For at that moment she had spotted her own quarry not fifty feet away.

Negligently holding a glass in one upraised hand and surveying the garden with a faint half-smile, Brian Turner stood framed in the light spilling out from the French doors. From the protection of the greenery under which she stood, Rowan stared at him, taking in his darkly handsome features and rangy, narrow-hipped build. His pictures had not done him justice, she acknowledged, and suddenly, despite all her suspicions, she felt the undeniable tug of his sexual magnetism. She thought she had prepared herself to be immune to this man. And yet the first time she laid eyes on him, she was responding like a trout to a lure.

Brian Turner, Rowan reluctantly admitted to herself, had the kind of lean male body that would look good in anything, but in the expensively cut evening clothes that fit smoothly over his broad shoulders and trim waist, he was devastating. No wonder he was so successful with women. As he stood leaning against the door frame and gazing lazily out over the fancifully lit garden, he raised his glass to his lips.

Looking away, she began walking slowly down the steps

farther away from the terrace. Somehow she was going to have to get an introduction. But how?

Rowan turned and seated herself on a stone bench in front of a manicured bed of white roses. It was an excellent spot for Brian Turner–watching. And over the next forty-five minutes she got to do a lot of that. He seemed on familiar terms with everyone here—both male and female. She saw Turner greet several Senate aides and wondered briefly if he were trying to charm his way out of his present predicament. But these conversations were brief. Actually, Rowan noted, he seemed much more interested in bantering with the ladies. As he laughed down teasingly into their receptive faces he had the lighthearted air of a man without a care in the world. *Just my luck,* Rowan thought. *In a few minutes he may pick one of these women up and take her home. If I want to meet the busy computer game king, I'll have to separate him from the competition —and quickly.*

With studied casualness Rowan began to glide in her quarry's direction. For the moment he was alone, so the opportunity was perfect. Turning her head so that Brian Turner wouldn't know she was even aware of him, she stationed herself in the line of his gaze and reached down, pretending to remove a pebble from her sandal. Would he take the bait? she wondered. With no false modesty she knew that she was just as attractive as the other women he'd been busy with all evening. But they obviously knew him, and she didn't.

Well, if he doesn't approach me, she told herself, *I can do something more drastic, like dumping my champagne on his jacket.* But that turned out to be quite unnecessary.

In the next minute she felt strong hands steady her shoulders. "Let me help you," a pleasantly deep voice offered politely.

Rowan looked up into the darkest pair of eyes she had ever encountered. They were like bottomless wells, and for an instant she felt as though she might drown in them.

"I hope you're willing to speak to strangers. But if not, I can ask our hostess for a formal introduction," he continued. "I'm Brian Turner." The words brought her back to reality.

"Rowan Strickland," she forced herself to return smoothly. "I trust April Coster's taste in guests implicitly." But it took all of her self-control to maintain her unruffled demeanor. Spreading through her was a sudden sensation of heat, as though she were a maverick asteroid orbiting too close to the sun.

"How have we missed each other?" her companion was saying. "I thought I'd met every good-looking woman in Washington, but obviously I was mistaken." She could see he was taking in her large blue eyes, curvaceous figure, and sophisticated hairdo.

Rowan's expression remained unchanged, but in truth she was disarmed by his directness. It seemed that getting to know this man wasn't going to be so difficult after all.

"Maybe you've been looking in the wrong places," she retorted sweetly, letting her lowered lashes mask the mixture of excitement and apprehension she knew was in her eyes. She could almost feel the adrenaline coursing through her veins. "I'm one of the nine-to-five set, so I don't have all that much time for socializing."

Rowan, as she regarded the faint laugh lines around his eyes and mouth and the glint of silver threading the virile thickness of his dark hair, was struck by his charm with an almost physical impact. His eyes had a way of dwelling on her face that was immensely flattering. "You need some more champagne," he remarked, casually reaching out and lifting a fresh glass from a passing silver tray.

Rowan smiled her thanks as she accepted and took a sip. She had played this meeting in her head dozens of times since her talk with Bill. But in her imagination she had never reacted to Brian Turner as she was now. What were they going to talk about? she wondered, searching her mind for some computer-related topic. But the ques-

18

tion was settled by her companion's next surprising comment.

"Does your foot hurt?" he asked with what sounded like real concern in his deep voice. "I've been told a pebble in the shoe can deliver a wallop out of all proportion to its size."

Pebble? Rowan thought blankly. And then she recalled her ruse with the shoe and nodded. Quickly she shook her head.

Turner smiled and waved an encompassing hand over the sweep of the garden. "Though I've always considered pebble paths charming, I've kept them out of my own landscaping and stuck to brick. But I do admire April's parterre," he added, referring to the elaborate pattern of hedges and paths below them. "I'm trying to do something similar on my own place in New Hampshire, but it will be a while before I can begin to rival this."

Rowan stared at him in astonishment. "You're interested in gardens?"

Turner chuckled in self-deprecation. "Yes, it was quite a struggle for me, choosing between engineering and landscape architecture. I like the outdoors so much I was tempted to go into garden design—on a grand scale. I wanted to turn the New Jersey cranberry bogs into another Central Park. Of course that was after my sea captain phase."

"Sea captain?" Rowan repeated.

"Yes, I suppose for most boys it's firemen or policemen. But I wanted to run away to sea." He shook his head and then grinned engagingly. "Common sense prevailed, however."

"Are you putting me on?" Rowan questioned.

He shook his head. "No, I'm doing my damndest to intrigue you."

Well, he was certainly succeeding, Rowan acknowledged to herself, returning his smile with a sparkling look. If she had met him under normal circumstances, she

19

would have found it difficult not to fall under his spell. He was so outwardly appealing. But, if her boss was right, behind all that warmth and charm must be a calculating mind capable of deceit and betrayal. *Back to business,* she told herself sternly. Bill wasn't interested in hearing about gardens or boyhood fantasies. "So, what career did you finally settle on?" she asked, setting her glass down on the stone wall bordering the terrace.

"Computer games," Brian answered. "I had to sublimate my yen for adventure somehow. And what do you do?" he inquired. His eyes were now looking down into hers with an unmistakable gleam of male interest.

Rowan didn't have to wonder what was going through his mind. Maybe he liked plants and boats, but she got the definite feeling he liked women even more.

If prudence dictated, she'd say good-bye to him right now before she got in over her head. But Rowan had a stubborn streak, and though she wouldn't admit it, she really was too intrigued to back off now. "Why, I'm just another bureaucrat—with the Securities and Exchange Commission," she answered—the story she'd prepared while under the hairdryer. In a way, she was actually telling the truth, if one stretched the point a bit. "And things are pretty dull right now," she went on, remembering how bored she'd been just this afternoon with the reports from that agency. "I'd rather talk about you."

"Oh, the perfect Washington cocktail party companion," Brian returned, setting his own glass down on the stone balustrade with casual grace and moving a step closer. "Well, the computer game business isn't all that interesting either."

Rowan looked at him with feigned disbelief. "But you're one of the men who've been pocketing all that money," she exclaimed. "The lunch hour crew in my office must drop enough silver in your mechanized bandits every month to set the Lone Ranger up for life."

Brian laughed appreciatively, the rich sound of his

amusement seeming to linger in the warm night air like a promise. "Does that include you?" he asked.

Rowan nodded. "Sometimes they do drag me along." That at least was true.

"I'll bet you're a good player," Brian said approvingly, dropping an arm lightly around her shoulder. Rowan was surprised by how natural the contact felt. Normally if a virtual stranger had been so familiar she would have immediately shaken him loose. She was intensely conscious that by not moving away now she was sending Brian Turner an unspoken message. That he had received it was equally apparent in the look of satisfaction that spread across his handsome face.

Keep your head together, Rowan warned herself as she gazed at him enigmatically. "It's the technical sophistication of those games that really fascinates me. How do you do it?"

Brian's smile widened, showing an even row of perfect teeth that glinted whitely in the pirate tan of his face. "Now I leave that to my design staff. I'm more involved in the business end of things now."

For the next half hour they chatted amiably. But though she kept trying, Rowan was unable to steer the conversation in the direction she wanted. Brian Turner seemed to be interested in everything under the sun including opera, skin diving, and the most recent Pulitzer Prize winners. Rowan found herself enjoying the give and take very much. She too had a wide range of interests, and she had met so many men who could talk only about their jobs; this one was a refreshing change. But she was also intensely aware that she was falling down on *her* job. *There's no use even trying to turn on my tape recorder,* she told herself. *He's the one charming me instead of the other way around!*

Picking up her glass, she took a slow sip, wondering how to guide the conversation along more profitable lines.

It was just then that out of the corner of her eye she

spotted a tall, lanky figure watching her intently. Rowan stiffened. It was Paul Burton—Bill's newest assistant. Clearly her boss had sent him along to keep an eye out for her. Unconsciously Rowan's hands clenched, and her delicate nostrils flared with irritation. Here she thought Bill had given her carte blanche, and instead he had sent Paul along to play nursemaid. It was humiliating.

"What's the matter?" Brian inquired in his resonant voice. "You've suddenly got a very odd expression on your face."

"I just saw someone I don't want to meet," Rowan volunteered.

"Oh?" Brian's eyes brightened, a smile lurking deep within them. "How about getting out of here then? I can show you what our company is developing for the arcades, if you want."

That sounds promising, Rowan thought, recklessly abandoning her earlier resolve to be cautious. She was determined now that having gone this far, no one was going to take this story away from her.

Still, as Brian Turner led her down the wide brick steps, away from the blazing lights of April Coster's party, she began to have second thoughts. But there was no opportunity to reconsider. All too quickly he was opening the door of a silver Bentley and dexterously settling her in its deep leather front seat.

CHAPTER TWO

It was one thing to be in the safety of a crowded party with a man like Brian Turner. It was quite another to sink into the shadowy, cushioned interior of his car and find him a dark overpowering presence as he reached across to pull her door closed.

"I always insist that my passengers wear a seat belt for safety's sake," he murmured, his voice warm and vibrant in the car's suddenly close quarters. "Let me help you. The catch is a bit hard to find in the dark."

Rowan's senses were electrically aware of the potent masculine figure beside her. As his long arm reached across her chest and pulled on the strap, she shivered slightly and then held her breath when she felt his hand hesitate on the buckle a moment longer than necessary.

As the automobile slid out of its parking place and headed for the open gate at the foot of April Coster's drive Rowan was definitely beginning to question her own judgment.

All too quickly the sleek automobile was pulling up under the canopy of the Wardman Park Hotel.

"My company keeps a suite of rooms in the residential wing here," Brian explained smoothly as a uniformed doorman approached the car.

Rowan shot him a sidelong glance, taking in the uncompromising line of his aristrocratic profile and the expensive cut of his dinner jacket. The man was obviously doing very well for himself if he could afford a suite in the fabulously

23

expensive Wardman Park. Was his money earned legitimately? Or was he unscrupulous in his drive to enrich himself? The question strengthened her resolve. *I know all about men like that,* Rowan told herself, *and they deserve to be exposed and punished.* She was not going to back out—not yet anyway.

In fact, there was no way, without causing a scene, that she could have retreated. When she got out of the car, Brian Turner's muscular arm wrapped itself so firmly around her narrow waist that it would have taken someone with a karate black belt to break his grip. As he steered her inexorably across the patterned marble foyer toward the brass-trimmed art nouveau elevators, Rowan was acutely conscious that the length of his hard body was pressed intimately against hers. She was alarmed by her equivocal reaction. Mixed with wariness was a large measure of feminine excitement.

As the heavy door of the small, old-fashioned elevator closed Brian reached over with his left hand and, cupping her chin, turned it up to his face. "Alone at last," he murmured, his midnight eyes plumbing the depths of hers. Rowan stared up at him, caught again in the mesmerizing ebony of his gaze. A girl could lose her head in those dark, intense depths. A responsive shiver ran down her spine. Despite all her suspicions about this man, there was no question that he attracted her in a very elemental way. She had never felt this strongly drawn to anyone before, not even Charles. Shaken by another twinge of doubt, she forced herself to look away. But as she lowered her head she felt Brian's lips brush against her hair and, despite herself, drew her breath in sharply.

Just then the elevator bounced to a halt on the fifth floor, and the door slid open. The spell of the moment was broken, and they both stepped out into the thickly carpeted hallway.

The apartment was at the end of one wing. Rowan had expected the decor to resemble a plush corporate head-

24

quarters, so she wasn't prepared for the elaborate jumble of antique oddities haphazardly scattered around the living room. Two old stained-glass windows and a rococo beveled mirror leaned against a wall. A massive oak armoire stood in the middle of the rug catty-corner to the tuxedo sofa. And, most surprising of all, a busty blond figurehead from an old sailing ship was tipped over sideways on a marble-topped mahogany washstand.

Rowan stood blinking at this assemblage while Brian watched her with amusement. "Not quite what you expected?" he inquired.

"Not quite," she agreed. "Are you also in the antique business?"

Brian shook his head. "While I'm down here, I like to take in the local auctions. I'm furnishing my house in New Hampshire, and I want it to be something special."

He moved forward and patted the figurehead's chipped blond tresses. "This lovely lady, for example, is going to brighten up my kitchen. I always did enjoy having breakfast with a beautiful woman." He shot her a grin, his eyes glinting wickedly.

Rowan stared at him, suddenly reminded of her harum-scarum older brothers. They'd always enjoyed getting a rise out of her with the same kind of teasing remarks. Spontaneously she returned the grin. "I never would have taken you for a fellow auction freak," she blurted. "I love the things you can pick up. That's how I've furnished my apartment, though I never came home with loot quite this grand."

Brian looked satisfied. "I knew the moment we met that we had a lot in common," he murmured. And once more Rowan was on her guard.

But the statement wasn't just the introduction to a glib line. "What do you collect?" he asked.

"Oh, mismatched stemwear, oak furniture that needs refinishing, and I'm looking for a set of lawyer's bookcases I can afford."

Brian nodded. "Yes, they're quite high these days. But I'm good at picking things up, and if I run across a reasonable set, I'll get them for you."

Rowan looked at him in amused surprise. Yes, he was good at pickups, she told herself. But, then, she'd been more than cooperative. "That's sweet of you," she purred. "But I wouldn't want you to go to any trouble . . ."

He waved away her protest casually. "Always glad to do a favor for a fellow antiques buff," he assured her, turning toward the bar installed between the double hung windows. Rowan watched his broad back uncertainly. He made it sound as though their relationship would continue well beyond tonight. And, on one level, she now wished it might. What was more, she felt a definite twinge of guilt about the deception she had set in motion. She wasn't here to be his friend—or his lover—as she was pretending. She was really here to uncover compromising information. In those circumstances it was painfully ironic that she found him so very appealing.

"What would you like to drink?" he asked, breaking her train of thought.

"Gin and tonic," she answered absently.

"Whatever you want is yours," he returned lightly.

If he only knew what she really wanted, he wouldn't have said that, Rowan thought. Suddenly more unsure of herself than ever, she poked her head around the corner into the dining room. There another incongruity awaited her. All the usual furniture had been removed and replaced with five brightly lit arcade games.

Brian looked over his shoulder. "I know," he acknowledged, "they don't exactly go with the antiques. But since the D.C. area supplies a lot of our business, we keep these on hand to impress potential customers."

Rowan glided toward one of the games, glad of another focus for her thoughts. This might be the opening she was looking for. Maybe if she was enthusiastic about his business, he'd talk about it.

"Go ahead and try one," Brian offered in his smoky voice. "You won't need any quarters."

Leaning over the machine, Rowan inspected the screen. It showed a monster spider hovering at the center of a web. Flying in and out between the threads were tiny spacecraft heading for the safety of their base. With most arcade games you were cast in only one part. But the beauty of this one, Rowan remembered, was that you could choose to be either the spider or the commander-in-chief of the spaceship armada. The idea had caused a mini-revolution in the electronic game industry.

Whimsically Rowan chose to be the spider, thinking it appropriate to her role tonight. But who was going to get caught in whose web? she wondered. The thought sent a cold shiver of apprehension and excitement down her spine.

Rowan was a natural player. But the combination of champagne and nervousness did nothing for her coordination. She ended the first round with only seventy ships to her credit.

Brian watched her performance impassively and then, at her suggestion, tried a round himself. Just as she had earlier, he chose to be the spider. But unlike Rowan he devastated the armada with cool efficiency.

"You really *can* play," Rowan applauded.

He sent her a sidelong glance, his dark eyes gazing at her with warm invitation. Yet overtly he was still behaving as though they might have come up to his rooms for a simple gaming session. "I get a lot of practice," he admitted. "And I did invent the game."

"Uh, what makes it work?" Rowan asked abruptly.

"Computer chips. You know, those tiny pieces of silicon that are taking over the world."

"Well, they must be pretty sophisticated," Rowan prompted. "Are they the same kind of chips that they're putting in the new cars to tell you when you need the transmission overhauled?"

27

"Similar," he conceded, turning toward the bar and picking up the two drinks he'd mixed. "But I'm not in the mood for an engineering discussion at the moment."

It was difficult for Rowan not to acknowledge the dart of chagrin that stabbed through her. Talking to the man about his business was like jabbing away at a boulder with a toothpick. Maybe there was no way of getting what she had come for and she was wasting her time—and possibly putting herself in jeopardy. After all, she was giving him every reason to expect that she'd wind up in his bed. And some men could become nasty when their sexual expectations weren't met.

Just then Rowan's blue eyes met Brian's with a little shock of collision. He was watching her closely. And as he handed her the drink he'd mixed, his fingers brushed hers with casual warmth.

"I'd like to see you play another round," Rowan suggested quickly. "Picking up pointers from a master is such a good way to learn."

He gave her a questioning look, his eyebrows beginning to elevate, obviously wondering exactly what game she had chosen to play. But his habitual good manners made him willing to go along with her for the moment. "I'd be delighted to share some pointers with you tonight," he drawled wryly as he sauntered lazily toward the Day-Glo–lit machine.

Rowan took a sip of her drink. It was quite heavy on the gin. Did he hope it would loosen her inhibitions? Well, she wasn't going to drink much, that was for sure.

"How did you get into the game business anyway?" she asked huskily, firmly back in her role of female sleuth.

"Oh, I was lucky enough to see the possibilities of these chips and get in on the ground floor," Brian replied, turning to her with another one of his entrancing smiles. "I'm good at seeing possibilities," he added smoothly.

Rowan already knew that. But right now her goal was to keep him talking.

"Well, did you ever think about using your chips in anything except games?" she hurried on.

His face clouded. "Never," he retorted, in a suddenly less forthcoming tone. She had obviously pressed too far. To cover her retreat she moved toward another machine and idly began to work the controls.

But though her casual position made her appear aimless, she was actually thinking hard, trying to figure out a way to draw some information from this maddening man. She was so preoccupied that she didn't notice Brian had finished his game and crossed the room to stand directly behind her. The gentle touch of his hand on the back of her neck made her jump, and she whirled around to face him, trying vainly to think of something to say that would cover her obvious discomfiture.

But the tension of the moment was mercifully broken by the ringing of the telephone.

"Would you excuse me," he asked, dropping his hand and turning toward the hall. "I don't want to bore you with business."

Tensely Rowan listened to his footsteps stride down the long hall and then the click of a door as he closed it firmly behind him. She would have been anything but bored if she could have overheard his call. Briefly she considered lifting the extension on the desk opposite the bar. But she quickly dismissed the idea as risky. Brian might well hear her picking up the receiver. However, she was grateful that he had left the room, as he'd given her an opportunity that she had been looking for. Opening her purse, she flipped the On button of the tiny tape recorder inside. It had forty-five minutes' worth of tape on what seemed to her an incredibly fragile little cassette. But it was the only model that had fit comfortably inside an evening purse. Was she going to get anything on it worth listening to? she asked herself with a doubtful sigh.

Her questing gaze swept the room taking in the odd assortment of antiques once again. And then as she

focused on the desk, a new idea took hold. It was obviously not a recent acquisition. Maybe the drawers held some
useful information. Keeping one ear cocked for Brian,
Rowan bent toward the desk drawers. Sliding the middle
one open, she noticed several neat stacks of paper. Somewhere in the back of her mind a moral voice was questioning her hasty decision. But she pushed the small attack of
conscience aside. Maybe what she was doing wasn't strict-
ly right. But it was all in a good cause, she reassured
herself: the protection of national security and, quite possibly, the advancement of her career. Besides, she told
herself firmly, if Turner had nothing to hide, then what
she was doing could cause no harm. And he would never
be the wiser anyway.

A messy drawer would have made her task easier. But
her host was obviously meticulous in his work habits and
would be sure to notice if any of the orderly stacks were
disarranged. Carefully Rowan began to sift through each
pile in turn. Most were quite routine—expense account
receipts, lists of company employees and phone numbers,
and party invitations. Fleetingly Rowan wished that she
could take these away with her, for she remembered how
well both Wally and Bill analyzed even the most trivial
material for important information. But removing anything would be a dead giveaway. What was more, she
admitted ruefully, it might compromise Bill.

While Rowan was thinking she was also inspecting papers. And the fourth stack her trembling fingers riffled
through yielded pay dirt. In the middle was a green slip
of paper labeled "Confidential Memo."

Rowan inhaled sharply as she scanned the message.
"Personnel reporting on strategies to deal with the Senate
investigation will meet at the Indian Princess, 28 June,
1730 hours." Elation surged through her. This was exactly
the kind of thing she had been hoping for.

Rowan had less than a minute to memorize the words,
for as she was replacing the green sheet in the desk, she

30

heard a door click open. Her heart beating inside her chest like a frenzied drum, she quietly slid the desk drawer closed and scurried across the carpet to the bar. Turning her back, she reached for the gin bottle. And as Brian entered the room she smiled brightly and put it down again.

"I was just freshening my drink," she explained untruthfully. It was impossible to control the exhilaration in her voice. She'd just put something over on this man, and the feeling was heady. She was trembling with excitement.

Brian paused, giving her a doubtful look. "I wouldn't have pegged you for a drinker," he remarked, frowning slightly. Realizing that she needed to distract him quickly, Rowan leaned forward, conscious of the view her low-cut dress must be giving him. His eyes gleamed as his gaze dropped to the swelling whiteness of her cleavage. "There *are* more intoxicating things than liquor, you know," she whispered thoatily, setting her glass gently on the bar. Inwardly she was astonished by her own brazenness. Was this really Rowan Strickland coming on to a man like a Hollywood temptress? Oddly, the alien persona gave her a euphoric sense of power. She had never before been the aggressor in sexual relationships. But assuming that role now with this man felt astonishingly good.

Brian responded as she had instinctively known he would. Crossing the room with swift purpose, he turned her body toward his, and pulled her into his arms. Rowan felt the brush of his lips on her forehead and the touch of a warm hand on the flesh above the low-cut back of her cocktail dress. She submerged herself in the pleasure of it gladly. She had just exercised a kind of feminine power she had never before dared to use. And the awareness of her success was more stimulating than any liquor could have been.

All at once she felt in control of the situation. She had pulled off her first espionage mission and covered her tracks as well. And if she could do that, she could escape from Brian Turner at the right moment—although she still wasn't quite sure how. But there was surely no hurry. In truth, she had to admit she was enjoying the touch of his lips and hands very much. And she realized with sudden clarity that part of her had been waiting for him to do this all evening. Why not prolong the pleasure, she asked herself, and see if she could learn something more at the same time? Again her mind registered a faint doubt. She and this man were attracted to each other. Was it fair to use that attraction to gain information? *But why not?* she asked herself. Successful men like Brian Turner were unscrupulous in using every weapon that came to hand. Why couldn't a woman do the same?

Lifting her head, Rowan gazed up at Brian, an expression of invitation on her face. The moment her eyes met his, any lingering reservations were quickly swept away. All evening she had been fighting her response to him. But now that it served a purpose, she might as well yield to it.

And his emotions were in tune with her own. "The moment I saw you looking so damned enticing on the patio, I knew we were going to wind up in each other's arms," he murmured gruffly. "We're going to be very, very fine together, Rowan," he added on a more urgent note. And then his lips covered hers.

Automatically she yielded the warm sweetness of her mouth to his sensuous exploration. As his lips and tongue fathomed hers, Rowan's senses were enveloped by a feeling like dark velvet. The hint of whiskey on his breath and the spicy scent of his after-shave seemed to whisper seductively inside her head.

Unconsciously her hands lifted to the back of his neck, feeling the crisp dark hair. Like everything else about him, it was vibrant with life. And being this close to him, she felt as though she were drinking in some of that strong male vibrancy.

One part of her brain sounded an alarm. But Rowan ignored the warning. This sweet intoxication was too pleasurable to deny. Although she had planned something quite different just moments ago, she was now responding to Brian as though they really had met by chance and impetuously decided to become lovers tonight.

All at once, she found herself looking forward eagerly to his next move. And when his lips left her mouth to travel down her neck, nibbling on the sensitive skin he found there, she arched her body against his just as though it were the most natural thing in the world, as though she had been doing it all her life. Her soft curves seemed to melt into the strong lines of his muscular male body. And she could feel the throbbing urgency of his desire. The knowledge of the effect she was having on him was as exhilarating as his lovemaking.

Brian's lips were exploring the line of her jaw now, dropping fiery little kisses that seemed to sear her skin.

"I've been wanting to do that since the moment I saw you at April's," he murmured.

"Yes," she breathed, her ability to think clearly almost totally obliterated. But his next words revived her defense systems.

"I think we'll be more comfortable in the bedroom," he said huskily.

To her shock Rowan found herself seriously considering the idea. Wally, she knew, would be more than willing to sleep with a potential informant. And in this case, she would be fulfilling her own needs as well as doing the job she had set out to accomplish. But her scruples quickly vanquished that temptation. No matter how much she wanted to, she couldn't go to bed with Brian Turner and then report to Bill in the morning on their pillow talk. It was time to dampen her libido and start behaving responsibly again. But how to dampen *his* libido—that was the real problem. She would have to do a quick about-face— and make it convincing.

Looking up at him through a thick screen of eyelashes, she whispered, "I couldn't sleep with a man I know so little about." The new role she had chosen was Little Miss Prim. But it seemed like the only course open at this point.

"But we've been talking all evening, and besides I think you know everything about me that you need to know," Brian insisted, his hands traveling down to her hips, where his fingers splayed out across the jersey-clad swelling and pulled her against his own hard body so that she could once more feel the extent of his excitement.

Rowan had to suppress a gasp as she felt his thrusting power. The feminine softness in her wanted desperately to yield to it. But she was determined that the new persona she had created would keep the upper hand.

Putting her palms flat against his chest, she forced herself to push him away slightly. Though he loosened his grip, he did not allow her to escape him completely.

Assuming her most innocent expression, Rowan looked up into his eyes, which now burned with the obsidian fires she had kindled. "Your charms may bring other women tumbling into your bed on such slight acquaintance," she said demurely. "But I'm not that type. I have to be more than attracted to a man to go to bed with him."

Brian's eyebrows began to pull together. "And just when did you make this little decision?" he questioned, an edge of irritation in his deep voice. After all, up until a few minutes ago she had been all compliance.

"It's not a decision I just made. It's always been my policy," Rowan declared with as much conviction as she could muster. "I believe in communication between men and women."

Brian sighed and then, taking her hand firmly in his, led her to the couch. "All right," he agreed resignedly. "Let's sit down and do some communicating. Exactly what else do you want to know about me?" As he asked, his fingers reached out to toy with a strand of her bright hair, and then he leaned over to bring it slowly to his lips. Somehow the gesture was explosively seductive. Sternly Rowan had to remind herself of her purpose before she could gather her wits to ask her first question.

"Well, are you in Washington on business, and how long do you plan to stay?" she began. This might be her last chance to get anything more out of him.

Brian's mouth curved in a smile. "Long enough," he parried. And then he whispered huskily, "Right now you're a very good reason for staying around." Leaning forward, he slipped an arm behind her back, and with his other hand pressed to her shoulder he began to lower her down onto the watered-silk cushions. Despite her earlier show of resolve this motion succeeded in sweeping away Rowan's power to resist, and she sighed weakly as his lips came down on hers again.

This time there was more urgency as he pressed the advantage; male instinct told him she was yielding. With infinite care he took her lower lip between his teeth, effectively silencing her. Before she was aware of what she was doing, her own teeth were reaching for his top lip and beginning to nibble in their own counterattack.

The effect on Brian was galvanizing; he groaned deep in his throat and one hand stroked down the length of her body like a conquistador taking possession of unexplored territory. Once more his fingers settled possessively on the curve of her hip.

Lifting his head, he looked down at her flushed face, and she could see that his own, beneath the bronze tan, was equally flushed. "Whatever you might think, I'm not in the habit of doing this sort of thing with women I barely know."

Somehow Rowan found this information pleasing. "Neither am I," she whispered.

"Then you must have felt the same attraction for me that I did for you," Brian persisted, with a surprising degree of feeling in the question.

"Yes," Rowan breathed, realizing as she spoke that it

35

was not a lie. What she felt for this man went far beyond anything she had experienced before—even with Charles.

The relief in his eyes moved her strangely. And she felt a stab of pain as she recalled her hidden motives. But he gave her no chance to dwell on the emotion, because in the next second his questing mouth was on hers again and she met his kiss eagerly, her tongue entwining lithely with his to increase their mutual pleasure. With burning anticipation she felt his hand traveling up to the low neckline of her jersey dress. Slipping beneath the clinging material of her bodice, his hand sought one of her breasts. She sighed her delight as his fingers delicately stroked the yielding curve and then circled the sensitive tip, which hardened under his sensual manipulations.

She couldn't stop her own hands from sliding open the buttons of his shirt so that her fingertips could graze over the hair-roughened skin of his chest. Suddenly she wanted to feel that masculine skin against her own soft flesh— without the encumbrance of his jacket and shirt.

Nevertheless, despite her sensual longings, there was a very real warning light flashing in Rowan's brain now. It might be more her fault than Brian Turner's, but this was going much farther than she had ever intended. And yet she was now almost completely in this enigmatic man's power.

With a tremendous effort of will she managed to tear her mouth away from his and her hands away from his shirt front. "I thought we'd agreed that we were going to talk," she gasped.

She saw Brian's eyes snap into focus on her face. "No, we just agreed to communicate. And that's what we're doing," he answered, his voice thick with desire. As he spoke he looked down into her face, his passionate eyes holding hers captive. And then slowly, tenderly, his fingers began exploring a path across her forehead and down her cheek, stopping to trace the soft outline of her reddened lips.

"You're one of the loveliest women I've ever seen," he whispered, "and I want so much to touch you all over." With infinite care he began to slip the top of her dress down from her pale shoulders. Then he bent suddenly demanding lips to the aching peaks of her breasts, where he favored first one and then the other with deliciously erotic little kisses.

The throbbing pleasure of the caresses sent a wave of fire coursing downward through Rowan's body. She could not stop him now; his touch was too thrilling to be denied.

"You want me. Admit it," Brian growled. And it was all true. She did want him now, and somehow nothing else seemed important. All the other considerations of the evening had been swept away.

Rowan opened her eyes, their blue darkened with her own passion. There was a high squealing noise at the edge of her awareness, but she was too caught up in the intense sensation of the moment to pay it any heed.

However, Brian Turner was apparently not quite so insensible. Slowly his head turned toward the origin of the sound. And then his body went even more rigid. In an instant he had levered himself off the couch and snatched her beaded purse from the table. The abrupt motion jarred Rowan from her trance, and she went cold with horror as she realized what the sound had to be. Her tape recorder! It must be malfunctioning.

This dreadful possibility was instantly confirmed as Brian jerked open the purse and extracted the small machine.

For a long, horrible moment he stared at it while a variety of expressions played across his face: surprise, disbelief, and then a gathering anger that tightened the muscles of his jaw so that his hard profile became chillingly masklike in its rigidity. As Rowan watched this terrifying transformation she shrank back into the cushions of the couch, her eyes fixed on his face like a small animal caught by the headlights of an oncoming truck. But his next move

37

jerked her out of her daze. With one economical movement he snapped the fragile machine in half, effectively cutting off its tinny screech.

The silence that now hung in the air was like the threatening calm that precedes a violent storm. Suddenly Rowan became vividly aware of her disarray. Hastily she pulled up the shoulders of her dress and tried to arrange its fitted front. Her cheeks burned as she struggled with the soft material, and when she looked up and found Brian staring at her cynically, she felt color wash over her pale skin like a red tide.

"As you can see, it's dangerous to rely on inferior equipment," he drawled in a voice that dripped with icicles. And then his fingers casually released the crushed pieces of plastic that had been her recorder. Rowan watched them scatter on the rug like a child's broken toy. She took a shuddering breath, trying to pull together her equally scattered wits. Nothing about this evening was going as she'd planned. She cursed herself for being an overconfident little fool. But regardless of her miscalculations, she wasn't going to let Brian Turner see how shaken she really felt. She looked up at him with defiance in her blue eyes. And then the defiance turned to outrage. He was calmly going through the contents of her purse. He had already removed her pearl-trimmed comb and matching lipstick case and was now opening her wallet with a maddening air of placid curiosity.

"Leave that alone!" she shrilled in protest. "You have no right!"

Brian's answering look was one of mock astonishment. "No right," he repeated disingenuously, his dark brows curving upward. "Don't you realize that using a concealed tape recorder is immoral as well as illegal? You've just given me all the right I need." The sentence had started out mildly, but the last words were snapped out between his teeth. He turned with an abrupt movement then and viciously flipped open the wallet. In a moment he had extracted her press card and, shooting her an icy look, began to read it aloud.

"Ms. Rowan Strickland, age twenty-five, height five-six, eyes blue, hair red. Well, we already know most of that, don't we." He paused. "And a bit more besides."

With a sinking feeling Rowan watched him turn the card over and began to read from the other side. "This certifies that Rowan Strickland is a member of the William R. Emory News Group." Brian's eyes slitted, and he turned toward her, holding the card now between thumb and forefinger as though it were trash he was reluctant to touch. "So you work for that scandalmonger! After I refused to talk to him this afternoon, I suppose I should have guessed he would try something underhanded."

Rowan leaped to Bill's defense. "This wasn't his idea at all; in fact—I was the one who talked him into it," she blurted. But the flash of disgust in Brian's eyes made her wish she could call the hasty words back. Why couldn't she learn to think before she spoke?

"You talked him into it?" he repeated slowly. "My God, what kind of female barracuda are you? Do you make a practice of selling your body for scraps of dirty Washington gossip?" He took a menacing step toward her, and Rowan instinctively shrank back against the couch.

"But I wasn't going to . . . to actually sleep with you," she stammered frantically. There was no way she could explain the tangled network of emotions she'd been struggling with while he was making love to her. It had not been her intention to seduce him for the information. But she had been attracted to him from the first, and her power over him had been intoxicating. His urgent response had fueled hers. And the combination had been explosive. But none of this was expressed in her stammered words.

She succeeded only in giving him an inaccurate picture of what had motivated her. And the incomplete admission seemed to enrage him further. He stared at her speechlessly for a moment while he took it in. "I see—you were teasing me a while ago—leading me on just so you could pry some information out of me. You never intended to follow through on the promises you were making with that cheating little body."

The last thing Rowan expected was Brian's next action. His eyes never leaving her face, he slipped his dinner jacket off and tossed it over the back of a nearby chair. "I've always prided myself on being a good judge of women," he remarked almost casually as he loosened his tie and then pulled it free of his collar and dropped it on the floor. "And I would have sworn you were really responding to my lovemaking. Either I'm a fool or you're one hell of an actress. Let's replay it again and see, shall we?"

Rowan stared at him wide-eyed. He couldn't possibly mean that, could he? But his next action removed all doubt. In one lithe motion he was beside her on the couch again, shoving her back into the cushions. Horrified, Rowan began to push at his chest and opened her mouth to protest. But that only gave him the opportunity to fasten his lips on hers and thrust a punitive tongue between her teeth. At the same time she felt his hips grinding insistently against hers while his hands went once more to the shoulders of her jersey dress. Real fear shot through Rowan. What had her foolishness unleashed; what kind of man was Brian Turner really? She began to struggle in earnest. But her feeble efforts were useless. Clamping her wrists together with one sinewy hand, he raised his body slightly and stared down at her.

"You've been sending lying little signals all evening," he ground out. "It's time you learned that eventually you have to make good on promises. And now I'm going to collect on what's owed me."

Rowan gasped and turned her head to the side.

But that only made him angrier. "Look at me, you little cheat," he rasped, seizing her chin with his free hand and

40

forcing her face around. "Did you really think I would let you get away with making a fool of me?"

Rowan's bravado had totally evaporated. Despite herself, her lower lip began to quiver, and as Brian glared down at her, she felt tears welling in her eyes. And then one leaked out and trickled down her cheek. Brian watched its progress with an expression of disgust.

"You're just full of tricks, aren't you?" he snarled. "I suppose you think that if you cry, I'll forget that you're a lying bitch."

But Rowan was incapable of answering. More tears trickled down her face, and she was powerless to stop them. They weren't just inspired by fear, but also by a profound sense of loss that she was not at the moment able to acknowledge.

Brian made a rough noise of disgust in his throat and then abruptly released her hands. She felt the weight of his body leave hers, and in a moment he was standing in front of the couch with his back to her.

"Get the hell out of here before I change my mind," he growled under his breath.

Rowan stared up at his tense shoulders in disbelief. And then, as his muttered words penetrated her brain, she hastily obeyed. When her dress had been set to right, she stood up, swept the contents of her evening bag back inside and then ran for the door. Minutes later she was downstairs in the lobby, tipping the doorman after he had hailed her a cab.

CHAPTER THREE

As the cab sped back to her apartment in Chevy Chase, Rowan could only stare out the window at the passing lights, her mind a frozen blank. She couldn't think about the scene that had just played itself out in Brian Turner's rooms. Like a recent knife cut, it was still too painfully fresh to probe. But after she had paid the driver and gained the safety of her own apartment, there was nothing to do but face the ignominious consequences of her foolish bravado.

Yet what were the consequences really? she asked herself. Despite the anger she had provoked, Brian Turner had not really hurt her. And, looking back, it seemed clear now that his intention had only been to frighten her and salve his wounded ego. She kicked off her shoes and stumbled wearily into the safe harbor of one of her blue linen easy chairs.

Putting her feet up on an oak-and-needlepoint footstool, she leaned back and closed her eyes. Usually the eclectic selection of antiques that filled her tiny apartment gave her pleasure. But tonight they only reminded her of Brian.

That taking off his jacket and loosening his tie bit was only an act, she told herself. *And I fell for it. I was scared witless. Some Mata Hari I turned out to be! I got in over my head and made a fool of myself.* Flushing with mortification, she remembered the hot tears that had leaked out of her eyes and trickled down her cheeks. *He must have enjoyed that,* she thought bitterly. *Just another weak and cowardly woman resorting to tears when her feminine wiles have failed and she's backed against the wall—or rather the sofa cushions,* she corrected herself ironically.

But the tears had not been just tears of fright, she acknowledged. In a way she had been mourning for the destruction of a budding relationship that might have ripened into something special under different circumstances. She had been strongly drawn to Brian. And that attraction had burgeoned during the evening, even while she was still calculating her moves and thinking of him as her quarry. But there could never be anything real between the two of them now.

The peremptory ring of her telephone interrupted her reflections. Picking up the receiver, she found Bill on the other end of the line.

"I was worried about you," his gruff voice complained. "Paul told me that you skipped out of that party with Turner. What happened? Are you all right?"

Touched by his anxiety, Rowan took the receiver away from her ear and looked down at it. Was she all right? She was going to have to be. Her hand clamped the receiver so hard that her knuckles turned white. Yet, when she brought it back to her mouth, she managed to speak firmly. Briefly she told Bill about the information she had gleaned from the evening's fiasco. His elation made her stomach knot. And she was glad that he couldn't see her stricken face. Pleading exhaustion, she ended the conversation quickly, promising a fuller report in the morning.

Yet, it was a long time before Rowan could get to sleep that night. The events of the evening kept playing themselves through her mind like a bitter song about love gone wrong. Finally, in the gray hours of the night, she fell into a fitful sleep.

The insistent twitter of her alarm clock brought her awake with a start. Groaning she shut it off. Her first instinct was to pull the covers over her head. But the more pragmatic side of her nature wouldn't let her. It was time

43

to stop feeling sorry for herself—and buckle down to the task at hand.

To bolster her mood she allowed herself a long luxurious shower. Afterwards she pulled a bright flowered summer dress from her closet and slipped into a pair of beige slingbacks before hailing a cab to April Coster's. There she picked up her car and then proceeded to the office to make a series of phone calls. By the time Bill slouched in, she knew that the *Indian Princess* was a large cruising sailboat registered in the name of Brian Turner and docked at the marina on Maine Avenue. Her boss's reaction was gleeful. "I'll get Paul to plant a bug on that boat," he crowed.

At the mention of listening devices Rowan felt herself go pink. But Bill was too preoccupied by the strategy his busy brain was cooking up to notice. While he paced back and forth, deep in thought, she mentally heaved a sigh of relief. Thank goodness he hadn't proposed that she be the one to plant the microphone. No way did she want to confront Mr. Brian Turner again! And, besides, her ethical qualms were growing stronger. Her behavior with Brian Turner and her ill-fated trick with the tape recorder had been bad enough, but a bug seemed like downright foul play. She thought of arguing the point with Bill, but she knew that would be so much wasted effort. And maybe, she rationalized, what they overheard would prove Turner's innocence rather than his guilt. Strangely the prospect was comforting. Even after the shattering denouement of their evening together Rowan had to admit that her preconceived opinion of Brian had been shaken. She wasn't so sure or so self-righteous anymore.

Rowan spent most of the morning listening to Bill and Paul making arrangements for the covert operation. In her present mood they sounded more like naughty little boys playing spies than sober investigative reporters. It was just lucky that Wally wasn't around. He would have made this caper into a three-ring circus. She was fervently thankful that her only part in the operation would be to drive Paul

44

to the wharf and keep lookout while he stole on board to conceal the recording equipment.

And so, that afternoon she found herself waiting in her car at the fish market parking lot, sniffing the rich variety of odors brought out by the hot July sun while Paul took a circuitous route to the marina through a nearby junkyard. As she sat and absentmindedly watched the busy scene on the pier, where every sort of seafood imaginable was being sold off the decks of permanently moored boats, Rowan pictured Paul's progress. By now, she thought, glancing at her watch, he must have made it onto the boat—if the dockmaster really looked the other way, as he had readily agreed to do after Bill's handsome bribe.

In her mind's eye she was just seeing Paul sneaking below deck when his voice in her ear made her jerk her head around with surprise.

The normally lively young man was leaning against the car with his head at the window. Beads of sweat dewed his upper lip.

"I hate to tell you this, Rowan, but you're going to have to take over."

"What are you talking about?" she asked, staring at him open-mouthed. "What's gone wrong."

Paul sighed. "It's my foot, believe it or not. The next time I want to sneak up on a marina, I won't go slipping through a junkyard," he said miserably. Then, to Rowan's amazement, he sat down heavily on the rutted surface of the parking lot next to her car and pulled off his shoe and sock. She could see an ugly-looking puncture in the ball of his foot. And as Paul squeezed it with his fingers, bringing dark blood to the surface, he winced.

"Just my rotten luck," he moaned with pain. "This is the first really big assignment Bill's given me, and I've just muffed it. I was almost through the yard when a rusty nail in a two-by-four got me." He gave Rowan a pitiful look. "I can hardly walk, Row, and I'm afraid what happens next is up to you."

She had been about to offer her sympathy, but his last words wiped all thought of his predicament from her mind. "What do you mean, 'up to me?' " Rowan shrilled, her voice spiraling up a half-octave. "You'd better call Bill and let him know. . . ." and then her voice trailed off. Bill, she knew, was in Baltimore for the afternoon.

Rowan's blue eyes stared at Paul fixedly. She felt trapped. Suddenly all her charitable thoughts about Brian Turner evaporated. The prospect of getting anywhere near the man made the blood drain out of her face. And, yet, what other option did she have?

Rowan leaned back against the car's headrest and looked at her watch. It was only 5 P.M., and Turner's meeting was hours away. There was little chance of running into him, she told herself. If she was going to go through with this thing, she would have to act quickly, before fear made a coward of her.

Suddenly remembering that she wasn't the only one with problems, she turned back to Paul. "That is rotten luck about your foot," she offered contritely. "I'm sorry. I know how much you wanted to pull this off."

Though the young man sighed, she could tell he was relieved that she had shouldered the responsibility. "Yeah, I'm going to have to take your car to the nearest emergency room," he said, "but first I'd better fill you in on what to do."

Twenty minutes later Rowan was standing on a narrow wooden finger pier looking at the three feet of oily water that separated her from the teak deck of Brian Turner's beautiful vintage yawl. She'd never make it across with high heels on, she mused, ruefully imagining herself floundering in the less than pristine water of the Potomac. Slipping off her sandals, she looked around for somewhere to stow them. Nearby was a large wooden storage locker bolted to the dock. Its padlock hung open. Quickly she lifted the lid and tucked the sandals under a pile of life

46

preservers. Then she turned back to the boat and tugged on one of the lines mooring it to the pier. It drifted a foot closer. "But not nearly close enough," Rowan muttered, eyeing the watery gap as though it were the Grand Canyon.

All at once her mind flashed on a vivid childhood memory of her carrot-haired older brothers, Michael and Tom, taunting her into jumping the stream in the woods behind their house. "Fraidy cat," Tom had jibed. And, furious, Rowan had made the jump on her short, six-year-old legs despite her terror.

"Oh, well, here goes nothing," she said aloud now. Tensing her muscles, she flung herself across the chasm and, unlike that earlier occasion, landed neatly on the sun-heated wooden deck.

Her small triumph was short-lived, however. What if she were discovered here? She was going to have to get the job done and leave quickly.

Planting the first bug on the far side of the hull just under the rub rail was easy. But the next one would have to go inside. Her heart sank when she tried the key Paul had given her on the main cabin hatch and found it didn't fit. How was she going to get into the cabin?

Nervously she began to make her way along the narrow walkway that led toward the bow. The teak was hot on her stockinged feet, and the deck swayed under her weight so that she had to hold on tightly to the rope railing. Thankfully the rich wood had been left unvarnished so that it wasn't slippery. On the other side of the cabin there was a forward hatch held secure by another padlock. Rowan looked down at her key. Bill had secured it from the dockmaster. But what if it didn't work on this lock either? Unless she took a hatchet to the deck, she wouldn't be able to get in and the job would only be half-done. Gingerly she inserted the key and gave the padlock a yank. Thankfully it slipped open in her hand.

For a moment she stared at the padlock in relief. And

then, anxious to gain the shelter of the craft's interior, she opened the small door and lowered herself through it.

Once inside, it took a minute for Rowan's eyes to adjust to the dimmer light. And when they did, she found herself in a small forward compartment full of white Dacron sail bags. Would this be a safe spot to hide the bug, she wondered a little desperately, or should she move aft toward the main cabin? That seemed like the better idea, and so she opened a small door and crept out into the craft's luxurious galley and dining area. It took her a few moments to decide on a spot, but she finally settled for the underside of a lower kitchen cabinet. She had just crawled back into the sail storage area and closed the door preparatory to making her escape, when she felt the boat sway under the impact of someone's weight. She froze with terror.

And then the sound of footsteps along the deck made her stare up at the low overhead and hold her breath.

The footsteps made a slow progress along the deck and paused just over her head. Rowan stared up in terror at the closed hatch. For a horrible moment she wondered if whoever was on board could see right through it. What if the hatch were thrown open now? She looked around the cabin desperately. Could she creep into the shelter of the small locker?

But the question was effectively settled for her when she heard a metallic click just above her head. My God, the padlock, she thought. Somebody had snapped it shut, locking her into this tiny prison.

Did they suspect a stowaway? she wondered. Or were they just locking the barn door, so to speak?

Rowan ran a nervous hand through her tangled hair, noting absentmindedly how quickly the heat of the airless cabin had turned her sleek coiffure into a mass of wayward curls. And her nerves were coiled just as tightly as she strained her ears to hear any sound.

The boat swayed slightly again, followed by the dull

thud of rubber-soled shoes hitting the dock. Rowan exhaled the breath she had been unconsciously holding. The prisoner gets a brief reprieve, she thought a little hysterically.

Brian Turner lowered his athletic body onto a narrow bench facing the boat and stretched his long, blue-jean–clad legs out on the splintered wood of the dock. As he pulled a pack of cigarettes from the pocket of his open-necked knit shirt he eyed the forward hatch cover thoughtfully. Was there someone inside? he wondered, lighting up and leaning back to inhale contemplatively.

A variety of possibilities ran through his head. This whole absurd issue of the wayward computer chips was certainly getting out of hand. Might a government investigative agency have gotten wind of the meeting he'd called? But how? And would they be incautious enough to try a little breaking and entering before the Senate hearing? It didn't seem likely—even if they were operating on the old "guilty until proven innocent" principle. After all, a foolish misstep could prejudice the case they were so carefully building against him.

But there was a more intriguing possibility. What if one of Bill Emory's meddling crew were in there? he asked himself, suddenly recalling Rowan's overbright eyes when he had returned to his living room after taking a phone call. At the time he'd assumed her excitement had something to do with himself. But now, to his chagrin, he had to admit that she might have been more interested in the contents of his desk than his lovemaking.

She might well have discovered the memo, he reflected. Then a grim smile began to play around his lips as he congratulated himself on changing the meeting time. What if that unprincipled but delectable little redhead were on board the boat? Would she really be stupid enough to tangle with him again after last night's ugly scene? Now he regretted his loss of self-control. It was out of character. But she had kicked him when he was already down, and he'd reacted emotionally. What a crushing disappointment she had turned out to be. He shook his head ruefully. From the moment he'd seen her in distress on the patio, he'd been intrigued and—he had to admit—more attracted than he'd been to any woman in a long time. She'd seemed like such a crazy mixture of temptress and innocent little girl. Somehow this unlikely combination had bewitched him. He had thought there was going to be something special between them—and not just in bed. There had been an alchemy when they met that promised to transmute base metal into something precious. From the way she'd responded to him, he had believed the feeling was mutual. But it had obviously all been an act on her part. And she'd left him with nothing but ashes. He stood up abruptly and threw his lit cigarette into the water, watching it splutter and die in the grimy liquid. Then he paced slowly up and down the length of the dock.

Ten minutes later three grim-faced men in business suits joined him. After they had shaken hands all around, Brian made a cautionary gesture and then drew them a few paces further from the boat.

"I'm afraid we've got unwanted company," he explained in answer to their puzzled expressions. "We can't meet on the *Indian Princess* as planned. We'll have to hold our conference here on the dock."

Jeff Armstrong, head of distribution, raised a pair of bushy eyebrows. "Is someone in there, Brian?"

His boss shrugged brawny shoulders. "I don't know yet, and I don't want to get you all involved. Maybe it's someone hoping for a free trip," he added sardonically. "And they might get just exactly that."

His associates laughed appreciatively, and Brian waited while the chuckles died down. "Seriously," he went on at last, "I hate to run out on you at a time like this, but I won't be forced into testifying until I know the whole story myself."

There were murmurs of agreement. "I don't mind holding the bag for a couple of weeks," Cleve O'Neill offered, raking a hand through his thinning hair. "But I've been on my feet at the Justice Department all day, Brian, and I need to sit down while we work this out."

His tall, dark-haired client smiled sympathetically. "I'll see what I can do. I think there are some flotation cushions stowed in this box," he added, striding toward the large wooden locker nearby. It too had been left open, he noted with a frown of irritation as he lifted the lid. But his expression altered after he had pulled out three of the orange cushions it contained. Underneath the last was a pair of dainty slingback sandals. Picking up one of the strappy little creations with an outstretched thumb and watching it dangle, a slow, wolfish smile spread across his dark face. "This certainly doesn't belong to Bill Emory," he murmured aloud, casting a gleaming, sidelong look at the boat bobbing gently nearby.

"Beg your pardon?" one of the men behind him questioned.

"It's nothing," Brian returned as he replaced the sandals and hoisted out one more cushion. "Just a little something to spice up my trip."

Rowan, who for the past hot and sweaty hour had been wishing fervently for a cool breeze and an iced drink, would have gladly endured another day in the ovenlike cabin to hear what Brian Turner and his cohorts were saying. But all that filtered through to her were low-pitched murmurs and an occasional maddening explosion of male laughter. *What in the world is going on out there?* she asked herself in frustration as she pulled the drenched bodice of her dress away from her sticky skin and fanned herself with her free hand. Of course it didn't do any good. Nothing short of an Arctic wind would do any good in this

51

inferno. But the heat was the least of her problems. She'd known that ever since she heard the ominous click of the padlock on the hatch cover.

She was in deep trouble. And very likely there was going to be a reckoning. Would it be like what had happened between her and Charles not so very long ago? she wondered with a groan. And then, before she could shove the painful memory back where she had locked it away, the whole wretched thing came leaping up at her like a monster from a dark cave.

It was uncanny how both relationships had begun in almost the same way, she told herself. She had met Charles at a fancy Washington soiree, too. And like the handsome electronics mogul, he had impressed her with his dark good looks and sophistication. Following their first romantic collision he had pursued her relentlessly, issuing invitations to dinner, concerts and plays at the Kennedy Center like confetti. And later there were flowers delivered to her desk at work and visits to his parents' country estate in Middleburg.

Looking back, Rowan realized that Charles had seen her as an asset—the right wife to enhance his Washington career. On his part there could have been few genuine feelings. But he had scarcely given her time to think. Overwhelmed and flattered by his adroit and persistent attentions, she had thought herself in love with him and accepted his engagement ring. Only a few weeks later, however, her pink cloud had turned brown at the edges when the *Washington Post* had broken an extensive GSA contract-peddling scheme. A group of suppliers had connived with the middle-level officials to sell the huge government purchasing agency substandard materials at inflated prices. And Charles had been part-owner of one of those companies.

Though Brian Turner had accused her of being immoral, in fact, she was very principled and was truly shocked by her fiancé's hidden breach of ethics and illegal source

of income. She had confronted him with the article immediately. But he only sneered at her moral outrage and
ridiculed her shock.

Rowan had broken the engagement immediately. And
there had been a terrible scene between them, during
which she'd found out just what Charles really thought of
her. The disillusionment and humiliation had been crushing. And the only thing she could be thankful for was that
her name had not been linked to his in the papers. Only
her friends and co-workers really knew. And she had put
on a false front with them, pretending that it didn't matter. But on the inside she had ached with hurt, mortification, and also self-doubt as she asked herself over and over
how she had let a man like Charles take her in so completely.

Rowan had promised herself that in future she would
be much more cautious about getting seriously involved
with a man. Well, she had certainly made a travesty of that
promise, she told herself. Because now she was very much
caught up with a man who was probably involved in something far worse than Charles's little government contract
scheme. If Brian Turner was selling his computer chips to
unfriendly nations, he could well be endangering the
security of the United States.

With a resigned expression Rowan lay back on the sail
bags and closed her aching eyes. If only this nightmare
would end! If only she'd shown some sense for a change
and refused to help Paul out. She was going to have to rely
on him to get her out of here now. How soon would he
realize she was trapped and come back?

At that moment the boat swayed again under someone's
weight and she realized that the murmur of voices had
stopped. Tensing, she listened as footsteps circled the
deck. But they seemed to be avoiding her hatch cover.
What was going on now, she asked herself, as she heard
several small thuds. And then her heart seemed to lurch
into her mouth as her ears caught the metallic grinding of

a starter motor. A powerful diesel roared into life and the boat shuddered. *My God,* Rowan thought hysterically, *he's starting it up! What am I going to do?* But there was nothing she could do, nothing but wait in spiraling terror as she felt the large boat begin to move out of its berth and then pick up speed as it headed out into the channel.

CHAPTER FOUR

Petrified, Rowan waited, feeling the throb of the engine as the boat plowed through the Potomac's summer-heated water. But inside her head the activity was dizzying. Her thoughts swirled like leaves in a storm. Who was maneuvering the boat? Did whoever it was know she was on board? Just then she heard once more the tread of rubber-soled deck shoes overhead. Metal scraped, and the forward hatch was abruptly thrown open.

Rowan's heart almost leaped through her chest. Was she about to be discovered? But the footsteps retreated, and then unseen hands pushed the cockpit hatch back six inches. At once a flow of air began to temper the heat inside the cabin. She lifted her face to it gratefully. Much longer in this closed cabin and she would have been cooked alive.

The engine droned on, and the craft moved swiftly out into the Chesapeake Bay. Below the flooring she could hear the gurgle of water as the keel cut steadily through the waves. Anxiously Rowan peered out the small Plexiglas porthole in the forward compartment. But from her unaccustomed vantage point she recognized nothing. Where were they going? she asked herself repeatedly. And how long before whoever was up there came below and found her? Was it Brian Turner? Was someone with him, or was she alone on this boat with the man whose angry attack had made her vow never to cross his path again?

It was hours later, as dusk began to quench some of the

light filtering through the small Plexiglas porthole, that the engines suddenly cut out. The almost eerie silence that followed jerked her from the uncomfortable trance she'd slipped into. A heavy splash and the rattle of chain told her the boat was being anchored. At once her heart began to bang like a kettledrum. Whoever was up there was bound to come down into the cabin soon.

As if on cue, the cockpit hatch grated as it was pushed back all the way, and then the sound of a horribly familiar masculine voice seemed to bounce off the walls of the enclosed space below.

"Don't you think it's time you let me know you've made yourself my guest?"

Rowan tried to swallow, but her throat was so parched she felt as though the sides of it were sticking together. She knew she should answer. It was ridiculous to try and hide. The intelligent thing was to come out boldly. But she couldn't do it. She could only stare helplessly in the direction of the taunting voice, her eyes dilated with fear.

The bodiless voice took on a note of caressing mockery. "Well, if you won't come out, I'll just have to come down and get you!" The boat rocked slightly with Brian's weight as he jumped lithely down through the open hatch. The door between the two compartments was thrown open. Instinctively Rowan shrank back, pressing herself against the wood paneling, but the movement was wasted effort. A sinewy brown hand reached out and handcuffed her wrist. In the next moment she was dragged without ceremony into the main cabin.

"Well, well, well . . . if it isn't the fiery little temptress with the defective tape recorder," Brian sneered. He towered over her, his coal-dark eyes savaging her. One hand rested on the cabin's interior wall to one side of her head while the other still shackled her wrist. She was effectively pinned between his lean body and the edge of the dinette table. The confrontation between herself and this man was now unavoidable, and its inevitability restored some of

56

Rowan's failing courage. She would not give him the satisfaction of cowering before him. Defiantly she lifted her small, pale face so that she could meet his burning gaze squarely. But the harsh tone of his voice almost made her lose her resolve.

"Just what the hell are you doing on my boat? Did that aging snoop you work for put you up to this?"

To keep her lips from trembling, Rowan constricted her mouth. But Brian's steel grip on her wrist began to tighten as well, so that her arm went numb.

"I warn you," he snapped between his teeth. "I want some answers and I want them now. If you're smart, you'll stop playing this ludicrous game. Because there's no one out here in the middle of the bay to enforce the rules, and at the moment I'm a very angry and impatient man."

He was right, Rowan realized. Defying him now was a foolish and useless gesture. He'd already put two and two together anyway. If she explained her reasons for trespassing, she wouldn't be telling him anything he hadn't already guessed.

She swallowed, then blurted, "Yes, it was Bill's idea." Though she was determined not to show weakness, her eyes skittered away from his. "I'd found out you were having a meeting, and he hoped to learn what it was about."

The information did nothing to cool Brian's temper. "So you *were* playing sticky fingers in my desk while I was answering the phone last night." He made a noise of disgust in his throat. "And all the while you were pretending to swoon at my touch." He released her wrist and seized her chin roughly, jerking her face up so that it was inches from his glowering features. "For sheer lying deception, you take the prize."

"I was only doing my job," Rowan defended.

"Your job," Brian bit out. "Your job makes my skin crawl. But if you're bad, your boss is much worse. If

Emory wanted to play Maxwell Smart on my property, he should have had the guts to come himself instead of sending a woman to do his dirty work."

Though in fact Bill hadn't assigned her to bug the *Indian Princess* and she was in this fix by sheer bad luck, Rowan gamely leaped to the defense of her boss and her sex. "There's nothing wrong with sending a woman!" she shot back. "I'm perfectly capable of taking care of myself."

Brian showed his teeth, but he wasn't smiling. "Oh, yes, you're doing a great job. If I really were the kind of ruthless crook you imagine, you could be in very big trouble, lady. What's to keep me from tossing you overboard with my anchor?"

Rowan flinched. But her temper quickly reasserted itself. "You wouldn't do that. You're really Mr. Nice Guy," she sneered, trying to jerk free of his grasp.

"That's right," he snarled back, the iron fingers tightening again. "I'm a real sweetheart. But you have a way of bringing out the worst in me. Now let's get back to the point of this interrogation. Just what exactly were you doing on my boat? Don't tell me you've got another malfunctioning tape recorder hidden on you." His sardonic gaze dropped to her bosom, where her perspiration-soaked dress clung, outlining the shape of her heaving breasts. And for a horrible split second Rowan knew her tormentor was entertaining the idea of searching her. But just then his dark gaze narrowed.

"No, it wouldn't be tape recorders." He gave her a glittering look of comprehension, and her heart once more flew into her throat. "You've been planting microphones, haven't you?"

Rowan averted her eyes as she felt the dark red color sweep into her cheeks. She was not proud of what she had done, and having Brian Turner catch her practically in the act made it a hundred times worse. She felt like some naughty schoolchild being reprimanded for petty theft. This whole scene was humiliating and degrading.

"How many?" Brian demanded tersely. "How many of those damn things have you stuck on my boat?"

When she didn't immediately reply, he shook her until her curls bobbed like tiny yo-yos. "Answer me!"

"Two . . ." Rowan got out between chattering teeth.

"Is that the truth? Because if it's not . . ." Brian's nostrils flared with the effort to hold his temper in check.

"Yes," Rowan interjected hastily. "Yes, I swear it."

Mercifully he relaxed his hold somewhat. "And where did you put them?"

His captive stared up into his tight features with wide, frightened blue eyes. Somehow she couldn't immediately bring herself to answer that. Her whole mission now seemed like such a complete failure.

"Never mind," Brian snapped out grimly. "I'm beginning to get a handle on how your twisted thinking process works. One outside and one in here, right?" He dropped his hands from her body and turned to gaze speculatively around the compact cabin. While Rowan massaged the sore spot where his fingers had dug into her flesh she watched him run an exploring hand around the benches and under the dinette table. Before she could stop herself, her guilty eyes went to the cabinets below the tiny stainless steel sink. At that moment Brian shot her a narrow-eyed look that intercepted the direction of her glance. Instantly he was examining the cabinets closely. With a grunt of satisfaction he yanked the bug from the underside where she had placed it, looked at it with disgust, and then dropped the offending object on the floor and ground it mercilessly beneath his heel.

Rowan winced as the costly piece of electronic circuitry turned into useless bits of broken metal. Was Bill listening in on this fiasco and cursing her inept performance? Would he ever trust her with a responsible job again?

Right now it didn't seem likely. Deflated, she sank down on the dinette bench.

Brian slipped the crushed microphone into a drawer, which he then carefully locked. "We wouldn't want to throw away the evidence, would we?" he asked sardonically.

Turning back to Rowan, he placed his lips close to her ear. "And now for the other one," he hissed. Yanking her back up, he once more pinioned her wrist in his strong grip and dragged her stumbling like a recalcitrant child up the companionway and into the cockpit.

Out in the open, Rowan blinked for a moment and then looked around quickly. If there were some sort of landmark nearby, perhaps she could shout a description of it before Brian found the microphone. That would give Bill a chance of locating and rescuing her. But there was nothing to be seen except the distant shadow of the shoreline on one side and the horizon across the broad expanse of open bay on the other.

Brian drummed his fingers menacingly on the teak hatch cover. "Are you going to tell me where it is, or do I have to shake it out of you again?"

Rowan scowled resentfully up at her tormentor. The man was a master of intimidation, she reflected bitterly. And right now he was winning. She felt weak, defenseless, and thoroughly beaten. What was the point of making him search? He would surely find it, and the delay would just make him angrier. Dispiritedly she pointed at the rub rail. "It's over there."

In two strides, Brian was out of the cockpit and kneeling at the edge of the deck to examine the area Rowan had indicated. But when his hand came away from the side of the boat holding the tiny listening device he did not immediately demolish it as she had expected. Instead, he leaned back on his haunches and gave Rowan a glinting look of triumph. Holding the mike up to his mouth, he spoke directly into it.

"I hope you're listening, Bill," he began, speaking calmly and deliberately. "Because this is to inform you that your busy little assistant is going on vacation. She won't be harmed, and if you say anything to the police, I will tell them that you illegally bugged my boat and bribed the dockmaster to gain illegal entry."

With a look of satisfaction Brian held the bug out at arm's length and then flipped it casually over the side. "From here on out, your big-eared employer can listen in on the jellyfish."

Rowan's frantic gaze followed the arc of the small microphone. It was her last hope of immediate rescue. As it disappeared beneath the surface of the water so too did her chances of getting out of this trap before Brian Turner could put into action whatever infernal plan he was hatching.

"What did you mean, 'going on vacation'?" she demanded, watching distrustfully as he rose easily to his feet and moved forward to jump lightly down into the cockpit. If only she could push him overboard, the thought flashed through her mind. But then what? She had no idea how to handle a boat this size, or even where she was, for that matter.

"I meant exactly what I said," Brian retorted, with a taunting little grin that emphasized how much he relished the idea. "I intend to disappear for a couple of weeks."

"To avoid testifying before the Senate committee," she supplied with keen suspicion.

But Brian was unmoved by her accusing tone. "Exactly," he confirmed, standing before her with his hands on his whipcord-lean hips and a small smile playing around his firm mouth. "I don't intend going before that committee until I'm good and ready. I'd expected to be lonely on this little retreat. But now," he purred with suggestive male satisfaction, "I'm going to have company."

Rowan's eyes slitted to points of fizzing blue fury. It was too much. Last night he had made a fool of her. And today he'd trapped her in his steambath of a boat, put her through hell, and quite possibly ruined her career as an investigative reporter. Now he proposed to kidnap her as well? Anger gathered into a tight knot in her chest and then surged upward so that her ears burned.

"I'm not going anywhere with you. Just who the hell do you think you are?"

He smirked. "From here on out you're doing exactly what I say."

Rowan took a step backward. "Criminal!"

"Sticks and stones—"

"Kidnaper!" She took another step, so that the backs of her knees came up against the edge of the bench.

"As to the first count," Brian shot back coolly, "you're still setting yourself up as judge and jury. And as far as the second goes, giving a stowaway a ride is not kidnaping."

The man was unbalanced, Rowan told herself as her hands reached backward and clutched the strap of a kapok flotation cushion. He was obviously on some kind of insane power trip and actually thought he could drag her off to some godforsaken hideout. And heaven only knew what he had in mind for her once he'd got her there.

He took an insolent step forward, one arm reaching for her shoulder. Unthinkingly Rowan reacted. With a quick snap of her wrist she hurled the boat cushion at him with all the force at her command. At that moment there was nothing in her mind but rising panic mixed with outrage, but as soon as her fingers released the cushion, she knew she'd made a mistake. Though Brian fielded the missile effortlessly, the expression that crossed his face was thunderous.

"You little fool! You deserve exactly what you're about to get!"

And what was that? Rowan's panic took over completely. Turning blindly, she jumped up on the bench and stumbled forward. But her calf abruptly collided with a wire shroud. The unforeseen impact knocked her off balance.

"Oh, no!" she managed to shout as her arms flailed wildly. But there was no hope of regaining her equilibrium. She was in midair for what seemed a painfully long time, and then she hit the water with a splat that knocked all the air out of her lungs. After that it was not Bill who was communing with the jellyfish that seasonally invade the bay, but Rowan. The hot, muggy July weather had simmered the Chesapeake into a salty fish chowder. And the main ingredient in the unsavory brew seemed to be wriggling, stinging sea nettles. Unluckily Rowan surfaced in the center of a raft of the unpleasant creatures.

Once, just after her move to Washington, she'd innocently gone swimming in the Bay and been horrified to encounter the blobby white menaces. She'd been badly stung on that occasion, and the experience had given her an unreasoning terror of the little beasts. That terror was magnified now.

When she surfaced and realized her predicament, she began to flail her arms and shriek hysterically as she felt the needlelike assaults of the nettles on her arms and legs. Her brain paralyzed with hysteria, she seemed to forget how to swim and sank once more beneath the churning surface, swallowing a mouthful of the unappealing brine in the process. Her full cotton skirt didn't help either. It clung to her thrashing legs in wet, crippling folds.

At first Brian watched this performance with a gleam of satisfaction. But his amusement changed almost instantly to concern. His brows knit, forming a black bar across his forehead, as he noticed the jellyfish and Rowan's reaction to them. The vixen deserved a dunking, dammit, but he didn't want her to get hurt. As she went down for the second time, he dove off the side of the *Indian Princess*. In three efficient strokes he reached her just as she bobbed up, spitting and choking.

Rowan felt a strong arm slide around beneath her breasts and gave another watery scream.

"Stop struggling and relax," her rescuer commanded. With one swift motion he stretched her out so that she was floating on top of him. And then he began to move back toward the boat. One arm sliced backward through the water while the other pinned her back against his chest. It was probably a standard lifesaving procedure, some part of her brain dimly registered, but the arm in intimate contact with her breasts did nothing to encourage relaxation. She was stung, badly frightened, and her teeth were chattering with shock.

When they reached the boat, she felt Brian's grip loosen, and for a moment her panic welled up again. But he quickly found a rope dangling off the anchored vessel's smooth white hull and curled Rowan's stiff fingers around it.

"Hold on," he told her. "After I climb up, I'll pull you aboard."

She could only blink dazedly at him and dart apprehensive looks around for more jellyfish. One of the creatures was quite near, she noted with another bubble of panic. It was drifting through the water like an exotic, sinister, pink-tinged flower. Rowan's teeth began to chatter again. Seeing the direction of her terror-stricken gaze, Brian pushed himself toward the stern, where the angle of the hull was closer to the waterline. Hooking his fingers around the rim, he easily hoisted his dripping body over the edge.

The man was in good shape, Rowan thought disjointedly. I could never do that in a million years. In fact, it was all she could do right now to cling to the rope which tethered her. But in the next instant that was no longer a problem. Strong hands reached down over the side, curled themselves around her shivering shoulders, and hauled her up. She found herself gasping in a dripping huddle on the cockpit's wooden bench. And while she blinked the water out of her eyes, Brian towered over her—a worried frown wrinkling his brow, his hands on his hips, and his thick, black hair hanging in wet points over his forehead.

"Are you hurt?" The tone of his voice was concerned. But Rowan was too battered and traumatized to notice. Fiery trails of jellyfish stings were burning along her unprotected arms and thighs.

"The nettles," she muttered weakly, turning her head away. Brian's gaze softened. He reached out and put his hands underneath her arms, being careful to avoid her injuries.

"Come on. I've got something that will help."

Too weak to protest, Rowan let him guide her stumbling and coughing back down into the cabin.

"First of all you've got to get out of that wet dress," he announced in a no-nonsense tone, his fingers already on the zipper at her back. Casually he slid it downward so that the sodden garment fell off her shivering shoulders. Convulsively Rowan grabbed at the limp bodice, clutching it to her breasts. Brian's hands stopped at her waist as he took in her fierce glare.

"I'm not letting you undress me!" she snapped.

He sighed impatiently. "You're going to have to get that ridiculous dress off. I don't intend to ravish you just now, if that's what's got you worried. You're not exactly a bathing beauty at the moment," he added callously, eyeing her limp coils of hair and smudged mascara. Rowan had a good idea how she must look, and the knowledge didn't improve her humor. She clutched the bodice more tightly, and her soft mouth curved down stubbornly.

Surprising her, Brian turned away and stripped his own sopping shirt off. He dropped it on the table in a wet heap and then pushed the dark hair off his forehead. The lean expanse of muscular male torso he'd revealed only increased Rowan's disquiet.

Brian had disappeared through the door that led into

the adjoining compartment. Three minutes passed, and then he returned with a white beach towel.

"Here, get out of your wet clothes and wrap this around yourself. Then we'll get down to business."

"What's that supposed to mean?" Rowan inquired. Accepting the terry cloth and holding it protectively in front of her, she let the clammy dress drop down around her waist.

Brian had turned his still naked back on her and was reaching into one of the cabinets over the sink. "Meat tenderizer," he explained. Taking out a recognizable commercial brand and removing the cap, he shook the brownish powder out into a small plastic dish. Then he added a few drops of water from a plastic container to mix a paste.

Rowan took advantage of his preoccupation. Quickly she shed her dress. For a moment she considered keeping her bra on. But the way the wet fabric was plastered to her body only made her breasts more prominent. So she kept on only her panties and swiftly wrapped the large towel around her slender body, sarong-style. She was just tucking a flap firmly in around her breasts when Brian turned, holding the mixture he'd prepared in one large palm.

His dark eyes gleamed appreciatively as he took in her deshabille and defiant expression.

"You look like Little Orphan Annie gone native," he drawled, making her turn a shade pinker with mortification as she contrasted her ruined appearance now with the studied sophistication she'd worked so hard to achieve for their first encounter. It seemed that Brian Turner had exposed her in just about every way possible.

But Rowan was in far too much physical discomfort to dwell for long on this minor irritation. She felt battered and bruised, and her delicate skin was laced with threads of pain where she'd been stung.

Brian's expression softened as his ebony gaze fell on the ugly red welts marring the creamy flesh on her shoulders.

"You'll have to lie down if I'm going to do this properly," he told her, indicating a V-shaped berth through the open companionway. It was the same one she'd occupied earlier in the day, only now the sail bags had been stowed in a locker and the bed was clean and inviting underneath the open hatch.

Doubtfully Rowan looked from the bed to Brian. He stood to one side now, holding the potion he'd mixed with an air of patient forbearance. Walking with all the erect dignity she could muster so as not to disturb the precarious arrangement of her towel, Rowan crossed in front of him. Once through the narrow doorway, she carefully arranged herself on the blue and white striped mattress.

"That's right," Brian rumbled approvingly as he moved to her side. "With your hands folded so primly across your chest, I feel like I'm giving you last rites instead of ministering to your ills."

"A few minutes ago you acted as though you'd like to see me dead," she pointed out in a strangled voice, her eyes averted from the tanned, muscled chest that loomed over her.

Brian chuckled unfeelingly. "You have some lessons to learn, Ms. Strickland. But I'm a man, and right now I'd like to do the teaching while you're very much alive and not covered by that towel."

While she absorbed the meaning of that, Brian took some of the mixture on his fingers and began to stroke it lightly along the sting marks. Rowan turned her flaming face further away from him. What he had just said made her even more burningly conscious of his touch. Dusk had fallen while they'd been struggling in the water, and now it was evening. A small battery-powered light shed a flickering illumination in the tiny compartment, and above her head the forward hatch was thrown back. Through the open square she could see the moon floating in a bank of cloud like a dented pewter plate. Soon the stars would be glittering alongside it.

Slowly, caressingly Brian's hands traveled over her aching body, delicately applying the soothing paste. The pain from her wounds began to subside, but wherever he touched her, new trails of a very different fire began to lick along her nerve paths. Despite everything, she was powerfully attracted to this man. And Brian, all her feminine instincts shrieked, was far from indifferent to her. He had insulted her earlier, but the insinuating way his hands soothed the ills of her flesh told a very different story. And the expression in his midnight eyes, she intuitively knew, would underline that appeal. But Rowan refused to meet that dark, compelling gaze. Instead she stared up through the hatch at the floating moon. The sexual tension between them now was a tangible thing. To dissipate it, she swallowed hard and searched her mind for some neutral remark to drop into the charged silence.

"How does that stuff work?" she asked huskily.

Brian's hand was on her calf. It paused for a moment on the smooth skin. "The nettles emit a protein poison. The tenderizer helps break it down."

His voice too was thick as his hand continued its downward stroking motion.

"Would you like something to eat or drink? There isn't much on board, but I could rustle up a sandwich and a cup of tea. And there's some brandy. I should have thought of it earlier. Would you like an inch or two of that?"

Rowan turned her head toward him. "No to everything but the tea. That sounds wonderful."

Brian left her side and disappeared through the small door, reemerging a few minutes later with a small cup of steaming liquid. Levering herself up carefully on one elbow, Rowan accepted the drink gratefully. But when it was at her lips, she paused. "How do I know this isn't drugged or poisoned?"

Brian's eyebrows began to rise slowly and a flush started across his high cheekbones.

"Okay, okay," Rowan said placatingly and then

downed the amber fluid in several hasty gulps to show her good faith. The tea had a pungent flavor that burned a path down her gullet to her stomach. She fell back on the mattress with her eyes closed and one hand on her throat while the other still clutched at the folds of her towel.

"I'm so tired," she muttered, already feeling the warmth of the drink spreading through her veins.

Brian chuckled as he watched her closely. She was a lovely thing lying there with her lowered eyelashes sweeping her cheek and her curls a bright nimbus on the pillow.

"Do you want to sleep now?"

She nodded and sighed. "Yes."

Quietly he clicked off the small light on the wall and turned to leave.

An hour later Brian had completed all his preparations for the morning and had gone out into the cockpit to enjoy a cigarette in the open air and finish the brandy. There had been no sound or stir of movement from Rowan's compartment, but that was predictable. It had given him a start when she'd questioned him about the tea, because in fact it had contained a crushed-up sleeping tablet. When traveling, he carried them as insurance against occasional bouts of insomnia. They were harmless, but effective. By giving her one, he told himself, he'd insured a tranquil night for both of them.

But now a worried frown began to pull at the ridge of eyebrow above his deep-set eyes. Maybe he shouldn't have given her the drug. He knew nothing of her medical history. She might have some sort of rare allergy. It had been awfully quiet down there for a while now.

Surging to his feet, he downed the remains of his brandy and tossed the half-smoked cigarette overboard. It was hissing when he turned to climb down into the faintly moonlit cabin. In two strides he crossed the main compartment and opened the door to the area where she slept.

Worriedly he scrutinized the outline of her prone body.

And then his expression softened to a gentle bemusement. She was breathing regularly; her white breasts, partially uncovered now beneath the loosened towel, were rising and falling with an unconsciously seductive motion. The towel had ridden up on her thighs, and the rounded pale flesh gave off an opalescent glow in the moonlit chamber.

As though he were drawn by an invisible silken cord, Brian came forward and stood at Rowan's side, gazing down into her face. Starlight filtered through the open hatch above her head, silvering her delicate features. A wayward breeze lifted tendrils of hair around her forehead. Brian's finger went to one of them, watching it cling like a living thing around his knuckle.

My God, but she was lovely! As he looked down at her, an undeniable warmth spread through his loins. Whatever she might be, whatever she might have done, he found her tremendously appealing. And, somehow, looking at her like this, it was impossible for him to believe all the things he'd told himself about her last night. Whatever her original motives, his instincts told him that she really had been responding to his lovemaking. Maybe she wasn't as reprehensible as he'd thought. Maybe she was just confused by her scoundrel of a boss, Bill Emory.

His hand went to her shoulder, feeling the skin like satin beneath his palm, and then he lowered his cheek to her breast and listened to the strong, regular beat of her heart. It was obvious that the pill he had deceived her into taking was doing her no harm. There was no longer any reason for him to linger, but still he stood staring down. Her lips parted slightly, and she stirred, the towel giving way even more so that her breasts were freed, their darkened tips just visible.

Groaning, Brian leaned down to brush the soft globes with his lips and then resolutely turned and left, giving her sleeping body only one last heated glance.

CHAPTER FIVE

Rowan's restless sleep was invaded by a high-pitched buzz that built into a metallic roar, followed by a thunderous *splat*. Her blue eyes snapped open, and she instinctively turned her face toward the source of the sound. Through the porthole next to her head, she could see a small yellow seaplane slushing to a stop less than fifty yards from the *Indian Princess*.

Abruptly all the details of yesterday's catastrophe chased one another through her memory like a cartoon misadventure run at high speed. However, the sound of footsteps on the deck overhead brought her quickly back to the very unfunny reality of her situation. She was the prisoner of a man whose ethics were questionable and whose intentions toward her were still a dangerous mystery. It was imperative that she extricate herself from this situation as soon as possible.

Suddenly she was very conscious that the towel she had draped around her body last night had slipped to the floor, leaving her dressed only in her lacy panties. What if Brian Turner came down here and saw her like this? The thought brought a hot flush to her cheeks. Involuntarily she felt a shiver of sensual awareness pass through her as she remembered the touch of Brian's hands on her naked skin last night.

Rowan looked wildly around the small cabin for the rest of her clothing and spotted the limp form of her ruined sun dress hung out to dry on a wooden hanger. Stained and blotched, it bore little resemblance to the dainty frock she had purchased at Bloomingdale's two weeks earlier. But it would cover her body. And right now that was the important thing if she was going to get out there and demand an explanation.

Quickly she reached for her dress, finding her bra hung neatly behind it. She had just dressed herself and was running nervous fingers through her tangled red-gold curls when the boat jerked forward and she heard the sound of the anchor being hauled aboard. What was going on? But the puzzle was solved a moment later when she heard the boat's engine kick over and then spring to life. Looking out the porthole, she watched the horizon shift as the vessel swung forward and then began to putt slowly toward the plane that had just landed.

My God, she thought. Obviously Brian was rendez-vousing with the waiting aircraft. But for what reason? Rowan asked herself, panic beginning to bubble up in her chest. Last night she had told herself that he couldn't go far in a sailboat, that today they would surely be discovered or he would relent and bring her back to D.C. But the seaplane outside put a much more sinister cast on things. She was standing indecisively in the middle of the cabin when she heard the motor cutting out again and the anchor chain playing out. Only now the boat was also tethered to the yellow seaplane.

She could hear Brian shouting in a friendly way to the pilot. They were obviously buddies. A sudden attack of nervous doubt kept her lingering in the companionway for a moment. She could hear the two men laughing together now. Were they laughing about her?

Suddenly Brian's tanned face and windblown thatch of dark hair appeared in the open hatch. "Don't be shy. Come on up and meet Hank," he invited with a wicked grin. "He's going to be flying us to our vacation paradise."

Rowan's jaw dropped open. "Vacation what?" she questioned, her voice rising in a small shriek.

"An island hideaway just for the two of us," he explained with great satisfaction. "I told you all my stowaways get very special treatment. At least the cute, red-headed ones do," he added, his eyes sweeping the fiery halo accenting her fury-reddened face.

Rowan's uncertainty metamorphosed into anger. The nerve of the man! Did he actually think he was going to drag her off like some helpless Sabine captive? Well, this was the twentieth century, and things like that just didn't happen anymore.

Outrage propelled her up the stairs and through the hatch to the deck. But once there, she found herself standing between two grinning and highly amused males.

"Well, well," Hank chuckled. "You've caught yourself quite a little mermaid here." The blond pilot's sparkling blue eyes surveyed Rowan's flushed face and heaving bosom appreciatively. "I wish I could share this little getaway with you, old buddy. But somehow I get the impression three would be a crowd."

At his ungentlemanly words Rowan instinctively took a step backwards and might have tumbled down the steps except for Brian's quick, steadying grasp. "Easy," he warned lightly. "You don't want to break a leg."

"No, that would spoil all your fun," she snapped and then turned her angry gaze back to Brian's companion. "Mr.—"

"You can call me Henry or Hank," he supplied helpfully.

"All right then, Hank. I want it on the record that I am being held prisoner by this man." She gestured at Brian, who was grinning broadly. "And that I am not going willingly anywhere he takes me."

The two friends exchanged glances. And then Hank shrugged and offered in a more sober tone, "I'm sorry, but I take my orders from Brian here. I know that if he's in charge, you won't be harmed in any way, Miss Strickland." He shot her a smile that probably never failed to sweep away all female opposition. But Rowan was in no mood to be charmed.

"How do I know that?" Rowan muttered between her teeth. It was obvious that this man was completely loyal to Brian Turner and would not offer her help. For the moment she had no choice but to watch helplessly as he and his boss transferred a few boxes of supplies to the plane and exchanged inscrutable remarks about people whose names she didn't recognize.

"If Blazer turns out to be the Judas, how will you handle it?" Hank asked as he stepped onto the wing holding a small crate.

Brian's expressive face darkened. "I have a couple of plans in mind, but I don't want to discuss them now." He shot a significant look in Rowan's direction.

It was only a matter of minutes before she found herself being guided firmly from the *Indian Princess*'s deck to the wing of the bright yellow seaplane. After helping her inside, Brian strapped her into one of the four contoured seats and provided her with a container of hot black coffee and a roll. Sulkily refusing to thank him, she averted her gaze. But he only whispered a mocking "Happy landings" in her ear and moved forward into the co-pilot's seat, leaving her alone with her churning thoughts.

What had happened to Paul? she wondered. She'd been counting on him to come to her rescue. But that was obviously impossible now. And what had Bill's reaction been to the threat Brian had muttered before tossing her ineffectually hidden bug into the bay? Would he ignore it and contact the police? *Or does he intend to let me take my chances?* she asked herself worriedly. It wouldn't surprise her if he did just that. After all, he'd warned her when she'd first applied for the job that investigative reporting wasn't "woman's work."

Rowan took a small sip of her coffee. The taste was bitter in her mouth, and the caffeine would only irritate her jumpy nerves. Yet the familiar beverage was somehow comforting. All at once it made her think of the night before, when Brian had offered her a cup of tea. Searing memories of the way her captor had stroked her flesh, ministering to her ills as she lay almost naked beneath his towel, only made her feel more insecure. She could recall nothing of what had happened after she'd drunk the tea. *I must have fallen asleep right away,* she mused. That surprised her. How could she have slumbered so restfully with Brian only a few feet away? And had the night really been restful? Snatches of dream images began to hover tantalizingly at the edges of her memory, and once more her telltale skin burned as she called up the feel of Brian's lips brushing the sensitive tips of her breasts. If she was already dreaming such things, how would she react to spending days alone with him?

She took an overhasty gulp of hot coffee and felt it burn her throat. The pain helped her marshal her scattered forces. Disciplining her wayward imagination, Rowan made a conscious effort to relax. Dithering and wild speculation would do her no good in this situation. If a chance for escape presented itself, she must be prepared to take advantage of it.

Instead of focusing on her own fears and uncertainties, Rowan turned her head from the window and began to listen in on the men's conversation.

"I've made arrangements for George to pick up the boat later this afternoon and return it to its slip," Brian was saying to the pilot.

"Don't intend to leave any traces, huh?" Hank chuckled. "I always knew you were a slick guy, but I never realized you had such a talent for intrigue."

Brian returned the laugh and leaned forward to light a cigarette. "I don't want anyone to know where I am until we've turned up some more information about those blasted chips. But I'll be in constant radio contact with you and Cleve. There's a ham set on the island."

Rowan's ears pricked up at that. She knew how to use

75

a two-way radio. Her father had been a ham freak for years, and she and her brothers had been using his set since they were skilled enough to chatter at the FCC-required pace. A set on the island meant she had a chance for escape. The thought cheered her somewhat, and she was able to look out the window and study the terrain flashing past beneath the yellow wing.

They were heading north. She could tell by the position of the sun. It was still quite early in the morning, only about seven, she noted, checking the waterproof watch on her wrist. Where were they going, and how long would it take? Steadily the sun climbed as the plane droned on. With a growing sense of disquiet Rowan watched fields and then foothills and mountainous terrain flash by. Had the pilot filed a flight plan? she wondered. She had heard no contact with ground stations. Brian was intent on making a secret of this whole business. So more than likely there was no flight plan that Bill would be able to track down.

The thought of being so completely cut off was sending shivers of alarm up her back. She shot a quick look at Brian's dark head. He was lounging comfortably in his seat as though he hadn't a care in the world. With a start she realized she wasn't really frightened of him. Some instinct deep inside her knew that he would not do her actual physical harm. Rather it was the attraction between them and the thought of what being alone with him might do to her that was frightening.

Gradually the monotonous drone of the engine, combined with emotional and physical exhaustion, began to do its work. Rowan's eyelids grew heavy. Several times she struggled to snap herself out of a growing lethargy. But finally she lost the battle and slumped sideways against the window frame into an uneasy sleep.

It was a shift in the engine's sound that jarred her awake several hours later. They were coming down low over sparkling blue water dotted with tiny, pine-covered is-

76

lands. Rowan's eyes widened as she took in the striking scene. And she came alert with a rush. "Where are we?" she asked aloud.

But the drone of the engine as the aircraft settled closer to the water blotted out her words. The plane hit the surface with a *splat* that jarred Rowan's teeth. As it plowed through the waves thick plumes of white spray flew up on all sides, curtaining the windows and momentarily darkening the cabin as though they'd flown into a cave. But the water quickly subsided, leaving a glitter of sunlight on the droplets left behind.

The plane turned and began taxiing toward the shore of a nearby island. Were they on a lake? she wondered, trying to fix a map of the northern U.S. in her mind. Or were they even still in the states? she asked herself, staring at the thick growth of pine trees crowding the shoreline. They were obviously quite far north. Maybe they had crossed over into Canada. Yes, that made more sense. If Brian were avoiding a Senate investigating committee, he would want to leave the country.

The transfer of people and supplies from the plane to the island was accomplished quickly. By the time the sun was directly overhead, Rowan was standing on the deserted shoreline watching in helpless frustration as Hank's yellow seaplane took off from the water, circled the island to dip a wing, and then slowly diminished against the cloudless sky. When she could no longer hear the drone of its engine, Rowan turned an accusing face to the tall, dark-haired man standing at her side. She had been a powerless victim long enough. It was high time she let Brian Turner know she wasn't victim material.

"Don't you think you'd better tell me what's going on?" she challenged. But to her chagrin the words came out with a quaver that undermined their intent.

Brian answered with a lazy smile. "All in good time. Let's go and inspect our quarters." Seizing her elbow, he

77

began to propel her toward a log cabin partially hidden among a thick stand of pines and sumacs. At first Rowan dragged her feet. But then she remembered the men's conversation on the plane. Most likely the two-way radio was in that cabin. The walk from the beach to the front door was no more than two hundred yards. When they reached the front porch, Brian produced a key from his pocket, inserted it in the lock, and threw open the heavy wooden door.

"All the comforts," he remarked, striding into a homey-looking living room furnished with sturdy colonial-style furniture. A huge natural stone fireplace dominated one end of the room, and a colorful rag rug covered the wide pine-planked floor. Brian dumped the duffel bag he'd been carrying next to a tweed armchair and then moved toward the small kitchen beyond the dining ell.

"Want something more to eat?" he asked cheerfully. "I can offer you eggs and bacon—even a steak if you're really hungry."

Rowan remained in the doorway, staring at him wordlessly. The sheer gall of the man was taking her breath away. "I demand to know just what my situation is," she clipped out harshly. "Is this the only house on the island, why have you brought me here, and just how long do you plan keeping up this ridiculous game?"

Brian extracted a container of frozen orange juice from the freezer section of the side-by-side refrigerator and then began rummaging in the cupboards for a pitcher. "I'm not playing a game," he remarked calmly. "I'm protecting my interests until the detective I've hired tracks down the real culprit in this computer chip fiasco." He rinsed out the pitcher and found a can opener to pry open the top of the juice can.

"Your situation is as follows: You are my uninvited guest on this delightful uninhabited island until such time as I see fit to return you to your usual nefarious activities in the nation's capital. Since you have no choice in the matter, I suggest you relax and enjoy yourself. And the first thing you should do is wipe that unattractive scowl off your very pretty face and get out of that ruined dress—which became almost transparent in the course of the dunking you took yesterday," he added, glancing up with an interested and suddenly all too comprehensive gaze.

Startled, Rowan stared down at the bodice of her sun dress. He was right, she noted with a self-conscious gasp. The material had lost its sizing and was revealing more than it covered.

"Juice?" Brian inquired politely, holding out a brimming glass of the sunny liquid. Somehow the commonplace gesture brought home her vulnerability more tellingly than anything else that had happened so far. She really was this man's captive, and she was going to be forced to rely on him for even the simplest needs. This realization made her mouth suddenly dry, and she reached out reflexively for the glass.

"That's better," Brian said approvingly. "Now why don't I see if I can find you something to wear." He eyed her bosom. "Have to keep things proper around here, you know. In fact," he threw over his shoulder as he disappeared into a short hall off the living room, "I'll even let you have the master bedroom. Can't say I'm not the perfect host."

Ignoring that remark, Rowan downed her drink and looked speculatively around at the interior of the cabin. Glancing into the hall, she saw that three doors led off it. If one was a bedroom and one a bath, the third might be where the radio was kept. She could hear, behind one door, the sound of drawers opening and closing. Was there time to try the knobs of the others? But before she'd taken a second step, Brian emerged from the bedroom grinning and holding aloft a pair of cutoffs and a T-shirt that bore the legend "Canada Geese Do It Higher."

"The owner of this place is an ornithologist," he explained, tossing the clothing in her direction.

In an ingrained response learned from her brothers she reached up and fielded the outfit.

"Good catch," Brian said. "I never did like sissy girls."

The remark came close to making Rowan grin. If there was anything she'd learned not to be with a gang of teasing older brothers, it was a sissy. But she quickly stifled the softened expression. She wasn't ready to be friendly with Brian Turner—not yet.

"And just whose cabin is this?" she asked guilelessly as she clutched the shorts and T-shirt against her chest. If he would reveal the name, she would have something concrete to send over the radio.

But Brian was maddeningly cagey. "Just an old school pal," he drawled. "Now I have a great idea. You look all hot and sweaty."

"Thanks a lot."

"Any time. How about taking a lovely, cool swim before you change your clothes? Just think how good that would feel!"

Rowan's blue eyes narrowed distrustfully. He was right; it would feel good. But she hadn't thought to bring a bathing suit along on her little boat-bugging expedition. And she certainly didn't plan on putting on an aquatic girlie show for Brian Turner. But when she said as much, he only laughed.

"You can swim in absolute privacy down at the cove. I won't peek. After all I've already seen most of you," he pointed out with graceless logic. "And if you're feeling particularly modest, keep your undies on."

Rowan shot him a murderous glare. But he was right on all counts. She really did want a bath. And she didn't have much to hide from this man anymore.

Five minutes later she was retracing her steps to the beach, a green towel around her shoulders and the T-shirt and cutoffs over her slender arm.

In any other circumstances she would have relished the chance to relax in this beautiful setting. It really was an

80

idyllic spot, she admitted, looking around at the crystal
blue water, set off so beguilingly by the brilliant green
foliage of the trees. The forest was full of wildflowers, she
noted. And the tall pines gave off a crisp, resinous scent
that made her nose wrinkle with pleasure.

Dipping a toe in the clear water lapping at the island's
rocky verge, she reveled in its cool touch. A cautious
glance back toward the cabin assured her that Brian Turner was nowhere in sight. Quickly she stripped off her
ruined dress and dropped it over a nearby pile of driftwood. For a moment she hesitated. Should she discard her
bra and panties as well? No. The situation between herself
and Turner was explosive enough. No point in adding any
more dry, or in this case wet, tinder.

The island's rock-rimmed edge dropped off in a sheer
underwater cliff at the waterline. Lowering herself into the
inviting waves, Rowan pushed off and struck out vigor-
ously for the end of the dock. But she couldn't help notic-
ing that her underwear really afforded very little
concealment. The water made it almost completely transparent. And the bra straps had stretched in the water,
hindering her movements. Treading water she peeled off
the offending garment and plopped it onto the end of the
dock before turning over on her back to float effortlessly
for a few minutes on the surface, her hair haloing out
around her on the water like fiery leaves framing a delicate
white water lily.

Rowan was in that vulnerable and revealing position
when the sound of heavy steps on the dock made her body
jackknife. Too startled to close her mouth, she swallowed
water as she sank beneath the surface. When she had
fought her way back, and opened her water-filled eyes, it
was to the sight of two hairy masculine legs dangling
comfortably over the end of the weathered dock.

"What—what are you doing here?" Rowan sputtered.
"You promised me complete privacy."

"Tsk, tsk," Brian countered. "A seasoned cloak-and-dagger type like you ought to know better than to trust the enemy, especially when it's someone as evil and sinister as you think I am."

Brian shot her a boyishly guileless smile. "Besides, I've brought you lunch." He gestured to the plate beside him, which held a sandwich and an apple. "So the least you can do is let me have a little fun for my efforts." Picking up her wet bra, he inserted a finger through the strap and dangled the wispy garment out over the water. "After all, we do have two weeks together," he continued amiably. "And we have to entertain ourselves somehow." Tossing the bra lightly in her direction, he looked with interest at the pearly white crescents that hovered just below the water.

Wildly Rowan clutched at the bra and began frantically trying to put it on underwater. When she finally emerged victorious, her wet hair hung down over her forehead like red snakes. And her eyes reflected back the azure of the water with a fierce blue light.

"Well, I'm not having fun. And I don't plan to entertain you. Go away so I can get dressed."

"You're cute that way," Brian remarked, pointedly ignoring her request. "You look like a Disney version of Medusa. But you're not, are you? Because if you were, peeking would have turned me to stone. And believe me, there's nothing stony about the way I'm feeling now."

Rowan's temper shot through the top of her head. "You get the hell out of here, or I'll stay in the water all night," she vowed.

Brian cocked his head with interest. "You really mean that, don't you? Aren't you afraid of getting wrinkles on those gorgeous breasts? Or do you know you can count on me to smooth them out for you."

The outrageous remark turned Rowan bright red. "You bastard!" she railed helplessly.

Brian held up one finger. "Language! Naughty,

naughty. If you want dinner tonight, you'd better clean up your act."

Without waiting for a reply he uncoiled his long body, stood up, stretched lazily, and then sauntered away while Rowan fumed.

However, her anger began to cool as she toweled herself dry. The teasing Brian had subjected her to was really no worse than what she had been accustomed to from her older brothers. And though their gibes could be merciless, they intended no real harm. Once again her instincts told her that Brian was the same way and she really was safe with him, at any rate, as safe as she wanted to be. And that was the problem, she admitted, vividly recalling Brian's effect on her the night of April Coster's party and her hazy erotic dreams of the night before. What would happen now that she was alone with this man who could turn her bones to wax and make her blood run hot in her veins like molten fire?

CHAPTER SIX

Once dressed in the T-shirt and cutoffs Brian had provided, Rowan did not immediately leave the dock. The clothes were ridiculously large. The shirt hung down to her thighs. And the cutoffs would have to be cinched some way to keep them from slipping down over her slender hips.

In no hurry to return to Brian Turner's company, Rowan perched cross-legged on the weathered boards and slowly ate her sandwich. When it was gone, she dusted her hands and stood up. Hitching her thumb into two belt loops of the sagging shorts to keep them up, she started to prowl along the shoreline, munching the apple Brian had left her for dessert. Across the sunlit water she could see a number of other islands. But none was near enough to risk a swim. Though she'd managed her fifty yards at the local pool, she was definitely no mermaid. *So I'm stuck in this Garden of Eden,* she grudgingly admitted, looking down in disgust at the remains of the fruit in her hand. What's more, if she was Eve, she'd already devoured the apple. Rowan tossed the core into the bushes and strode on.

The shoreline beyond the protective cove curved away in a fairly tight circle. And from its curvature Rowan judged that Brian's island was no more than a few hundred acres. Where were they? she asked herself again. As far as she knew, they had flown straight north. And the island's delightfully temperate summer weather, after the steambath that was Washington in late July, confirmed her guess about their latitude.

What else did she know about this place? Rowan asked herself. Well, for one thing she had noticed a current while swimming. Perhaps the island was situated not in a lake, but in a large river. And the island seemed to have a strong base of dark rock, judging from the appearance of the waterline and the rounded outcroppings breaking through the soil at frequent intervals.

However, her geography was weak enough to forestall further speculation. Trying to trick Brian into revealing their location seemed the more profitable tack. Just then Rowan came to an abrupt halt. Beyond the rise to her right she had spotted a radio antenna. At once all her senses were on the alert. She'd been wondering where that ham radio was kept and had speculated it was in the cabin. But obviously she'd been mistaken.

Taking a quick look around to make sure her captor was nowhere in sight, she left the water's edge and scrambled up into the rough ground, heading in the direction of the antenna. It was uphill all the way, but there was a faint path to follow where other feet had broken the trail. *Brian's?* More likely, the tracks belonged to the owner of this place. She'd have to find an opportunity to look through the clothes stored in her room. Maybe she'd find a name tag to identify Brian's mysterious friend.

It was only a matter of minutes before Rowan broke into a small clearing dominated by a shed with an outside generator. The antenna she'd spotted was on the roof. There could be no doubt now, Rowan told herself as she eyed her find with triumphant eyes. This was the radio. But, to her disappointment, when she tried the solidly built door, it was locked securely and no amount of jiggling and thumping was going to open it. Several times she went to the small window and peered in. It was too dark to see much, but what she could make out confirmed her belief that if she could find the key to this place she had a chance yet to show Mr. Brian Turner just what a determined woman could do.

An hour later Rowan meandered back to the cottage. Her hand still twined in the loops at her waist, she had literally and figuratively girded up her loins for another encounter with her host. But to her immense relief he was nowhere in sight. Seizing the opportunity, Rowan made for the bedroom Brian had offered earlier in the day, locked the door firmly behind her, and leaned against the sturdy pine crossbeam with a sigh of relief. The room was as rustic as the rest of the cabin, with knotty-pine paneling on the walls, a hand-stitched patchwork quilt on the bed, and muslin curtains at the window. Drawing them quickly across the brass rod, Rowan set about sifting through the sweaters, T-shirts, and jeans folded in the large bureau. But she drew a blank. It wasn't until she went to the closet and began flicking through its contents that she came up with something useful. There were no name tags in the clothes hung there, but she did find a letter in an old windbreaker on the hook. The date on the postmark was a year old, and the letter was addressed to a Professor Lawrence Gustavson, chairman of the biology department at a prominent Canadian university. Rowan was elated. Gustavson was an unusual name, and if he owned this island, that would be recorded along with its location. If she could get to that radio, she might well have enough information now for Bill to go on.

At that moment Rowan's jubilation was interrupted by the sound of pots and pans clattering outside in the kitchen. She eyed the door nervously. Brian must be rattling them deliberately. He'd probably assumed she was napping behind this closed door. Quickly restoring the envelope to the windbreaker at the back of the closet, Rowan tucked in the ends of her overlong T-shirt and cautiously unlocked the bedroom door.

When she entered the combination kitchen–living room, Brian Turner was busy scrubbing potatoes. He too was wearing faded cutoffs. Only his fit closely over his narrow waist and firm buttocks. As he reached for the salt in an upper cabinet Rowan took in the ripple of sinew on his tan, solidly muscled legs. Forcing her eyes upward, she noted with wry amusement that his shirt far outclassed hers. It was a soft yellow knit that shrieked money and status. This man might like to rough it, but he liked to rough it in style.

"Oh, there you are, lazybones," he called casually over his shoulder. "I figured we might as well have an early dinner. You're just in time to help. I caught some bass, and I'll clean and grill them in the fireplace, if you finish these potatoes and find a green vegetable in the freezer. I discovered some watercress that we can use for a garnish. And there are wild raspberries we can pick for dessert."

Startled by his obvious enthusiasm, Rowan gawked for a moment while she took in the new situation. Apparently he was no longer in a teasing mood and had instead adopted an air of jovial companionship. But they weren't companions. She was his prisoner. And no amount of playacting would change that adversary relationship. On the other hand, she might as well go along with his affable mood and hope it would last until she could get herself out of her predicament. You can catch more flies with honey than you can with vinegar, she reminded herself, calling to mind the aphorism her mother had always chided her with when she fought her brothers. Maybe if she was pleasant, Brian would inadvertently drop some tidbit of useful information.

"I'll be happy to help," she offered, assuming an innocent smile and gliding forward. "But it's a little difficult to work in the kitchen with only one hand." She gestured meaningfully at the belt loops she was holding firmly with her thumb and forefinger.

Brian's smile was equally guileless. "Well, let me take care of that right now," he offered, rummaging in a lower drawer and turning triumphantly with a short length of clothesline. "I don't know what Larry used this for, but I'm sure he won't mind our turning it into a belt."

So his friend's name *was* Larry. That probably meant the name on the envelope was correct. Rowan's quick mind filed this new bit of information away for future reference. But her powers of deductive reasoning were scattered when Brian crossed the room and reached down to span the width of her narrow waist with his large hands.

"Such a tiny little waist," he murmured, his breath feathering the top of her head as his hands lingered on her body. "I can see why you're having trouble." His nearness was as unsettling as a boulder tossed into a tranquil pool. It was all Rowan could do to keep from trembling as his lean fingers threaded the rope through the belt loops. "I think a square knot would keep it most secure," he murmured in his smoky voice. "But I never could tie one of those backwards," he added, slipping around in back of her and circling her ribs with his long arms. As his hands moved toward her waist his arms casually brushed against the swell of her breasts beneath the ridiculous T-shirt. And this time she did tremble.

"Steady now," Brian cautioned. "It'll take twice as long if you don't keep absolutely still. I'm a terrible fumble-fingers."

Rowan went rigid as a statue and held her breath. *Fumble-fingers, my eye!* He was a practiced seducer clearly enjoying trying out his wiles on her. What was most maddening about his ploy was the effect it was having. Although the rational part of her mind knew exactly what he was up to, the feminine core of her was responding like one of his programmed computer games.

"There now," he commented cheerfully, giving her waistline a last proprietary pat. "Doesn't that do the trick for you?"

"Just great," Rowan agreed through her teeth. Although she knew he had to be aware of her mixed emotions, she refused to give him an opening to tease her.

"Now, how can I help with dinner?" she inquired sweetly.

"Better do the potatoes first. Wrap them in foil and I'll bury them in the coals. When that's done, I'll show you the raspberry patch."

The meal, when it was finally brought forth through their combined efforts, turned out surprisingly well. In addition to the watercress, Brian had found a small green leaf that imparted a delicate lemon bouquet to the bass. And the tart, juicy raspberries were the perfect way to end their repast. Brian had even produced an excellent bottle of dry white wine to complement the fish.

"To make good use of the old cliché, how does a nice girl like you get involved in cloak-and-dagger work?" Brian asked, pushing his empty berry bowl to the side.

Rowan glanced up sharply. Was he trying to start something? But his open expression made the question merely conversational. She answered lightly. "In high school I idolized Woodward and Bernstein. And when I was a senior, majoring in journalism, at Oregon State, Bill came out there on a speaking tour. I stayed after his lecture to talk to him. I've always admired his work. You may think he's treated you badly, but he really has uncovered major misuses of power in the capital. Anyway," she rushed on before Brian could voice an opinion about her boss, "he advised me to get some newspaper experience under my belt before I tried investigative reporting. I took his advice and found a job on a small-town weekly. But reporting on the town council meetings and chili cookoffs was really tame. So after a couple of years I quit and headed for Washington. Bill didn't fall all over himself to give me a job. He'd never hired a woman as an investigative reporter before, so it took a lot of convincing. But finally he agreed to give me a chance."

"Then you've always been the enterprising type," Brian suggested, leaning back lazily in his chair.

"I had to be," Rowan flared. "I wasn't the eldest son of a rich family like you."

"Ouch," he retorted. "I see you've been checking me out in the scandal sheets." He leered outrageously. "Well, sometimes being the eldest son in a rich family isn't all roses. People were comparing my performance to my father's before I started grade school. And when I broke away from the family tradition to start my own business, my parents practically went into mourning."

"Yes," Rowan answered his original question, "I wouldn't stage a meeting like ours unless I had thoroughly researched the uh . . ."

"Pigeon," Brian supplied.

Rowan had the decency to blush. But doing her best to ignore the barb, she plunged on. "Your parents may have gone into mourning. But you still had your million-dollar trust fund when you needed the money to start a business of your own. In my family it was the boys who got the financial support. I had to commute to Oregon State. They went to Stanford or Berkeley in style."

"Don't shoot, lady." Brian held up his palms as though she had him at gunpoint. "That's quite a chip you have on your shoulder." One of his hands dropped and lightly brushed her upper arm, unnecessarily curling around her back for a second before returning to his wineglass on the table.

But even that brief contact had its effect on Rowan. Her skin tingled where he'd touched her. And once more she was blazingly aware of the attraction between them. He was showing her once more the easy charm she remembered from that first night at April Coster's. It had disarmed her then, and she was no more immune to it now. *Careful, Rowan,* she warned herself.

To conceal her discomfiture, she picked up her own wineglass and looked down into its pale depths.

But his next words made her glance up quickly.

"I've just figured something out," he announced with

mock sagacity. "Your brothers are responsible for all your harebrained stunts. You're still competing with them—and trying to live up to the tomboy standards they set for you when you were still the fifth wheel in the Strickland family."

Rowan began to bristle. In other circumstances she might have been amused. But now she deliberately channeled her fear of this man's effect on her into defensive anger. "I would have expected more from you," she shot back. "That's a pretty simplistic explanation. Surely by now you've learned that people are more complicated than that."

"Sometimes. But sometimes things that seem complicated are really simple. You, for example, are a beautiful and intelligent woman." His voice deepened. "You don't need to compete with men when you can so easily devastate them." With casual assurance his hand went to her chin and tipped it up so that he could smile directly into her widening blue eyes. By the light of the setting sun she could see her own image reflected on his pupils and stared at its fiery imprint helplessly. "Rowan Strickland," he crooned, "do you understand the effect you're having on me right now? It's not a question of competition, but of completion. We were meant to complement each other, Rowan, in the most basic sense. But you already know that, don't you?"

Dry-mouthed, Rowan watched as he stood up and calmly removed her glass from her loosened fingers. Then, with one swift motion, he pulled her onto her feet and into his arms.

She opened her mouth to protest. But Brian took her parted lips as an opportunity. Swiftly his own lips descended to meet hers in a kiss that was as masterful as it was passionate. Forgotten were the baiting words she had intended to hurl at him, as his tongue darted into the moist sweetness of her mouth, drawing a response that surprised her with its intensity. Of their own volition her hands wound themselves around his neck and slid upward to tangle themselves in the thick hair at the back of his head.

At first she simply clung to him, enjoying his sensuous exploration of her mouth, the feel of his strong hands as they caressed her back, the aromatic scent of woodsmoke that clung to his clothing.

But she could not remain passive for long. Like a hummingbird dipping after honey, her own tongue sprang forward to meet his. And her hands moved to explore the sides of his face and the planes of his high cheekbones, taking tactile delight in the feel of his skin under her fingertips.

She heard him sigh with pleasure at the touch. And then he was shifting her body so that one hand could cup her right breast through the soft material of her T-shirt. He recognized her deep response not just by her sigh of pleasure but by the way her nipple hardened in his palm. Slowly he began to stroke the firm peak of throbbing sensation with his thumb, and then he bent to find it with his lips. In answer Rowan trembled, caught up in the tide of sensuality he was unleashing within her body.

"Your clothes are in the way," he whispered hoarsely, reaching behind her to unhook her bra, then his hands returned eagerly to her breasts. Rowan moaned as he stroked and caressed her passion-sensitive skin. And when he gently took her nipples between his thumbs and index fingers, she threw her head back and arched her body toward him—glorying in the exquisite sensations he was creating.

But as he began to pull her shirt over her head her eyes snapped open. What was she doing? she asked herself and then sardonically answered her own silent question. She was falling under Brian Turner's spell again. And she couldn't allow it to happen.

"Please," she whispered. "Don't do this to me."

Brian paused and lifted his head to stare questioningly down into her flushed face. What he read there seemed to dampen his ardor. To her surprise, he dropped the edge of her shirt and took a step backward. She could see the play of emotions across his strong features as he struggled for control. "You're right," he acknowledged finally, the words escaping his lips in a regretful sigh. "I'm not playing fair."

Rowan turned away. Head bowed, she put her clothing back in order, hoping Brian wasn't looking.

Behind her she heard the clink of crockery being stacked.

"Let's get the dishes done," he suggested evenly.

Glad for a simple activity to focus on, Rowan began to help him clear the table.

As they finished drying the dishes it grew dark, and Brian put down his towel to light several kerosene lamps.

Rowan watched with interest. "If there's no electricity here, what do the appliances run on?" she asked and then almost bit her tongue as she remembered the generator outside the radio shed. But Brian didn't notice her small lapse.

"Bottled gas. But the water has to be pumped by hand into a cistern. So if you use too much when you shower tomorrow, I'll put you on pumping duty."

After the sun set, the temperature dropped, and Brian set about stoking up the fire. Rowan watched him skillfully lay more wood on the dying coals. The dry wood caught almost immediately. And soon flames were dancing in the fireplace and casting flickering shadows about the homey room.

The romantic setting made her conscious once again of just how isolated this cabin was. Shivering, she hugged her shoulders, watching Brian through lowered lashes. He had backed off when his lovemaking had alarmed her awhile ago. But that had been entirely his choice. What if he hadn't stopped? What would have happened then? She was at his mercy here.

After seeing to the fire, Brian settled down in one of the

armchairs facing the hearth and lit a cigarette. Rowan hesitantly chose the chair across from him.

Exhaling a thin wreath of blue smoke, he looked up and smiled. "It's been quite an eventful day."

Rowan nodded. "That's the understatement of the year."

"I guess you're right," he acknowledged, leaning back into the deep cushions. "But from now on, it's going to be a low-key vacation. Think of it as R and R."

"Courtesy of Turner Electronics," Rowan couldn't help adding.

"Don't go spoiling the peace and tranquility," Brian advised. "We've left the real world behind. There are only the two of us here, in a little world of our own. And I suggest we try to get along with each other—or it'll be a long two weeks."

Rowan could see the merits of his suggestion. Besides, he held all the cards. Unless she could get to that radio, she was stuck here for the duration.

"All right, a truce, then," she suggested.

"Yes. A truce."

They sat in the flickering firelight for several silent moments then. And Rowan couldn't help stifling a yawn.

"As I said, it's been a rather full day," Brian told her. "Better get to bed."

Standing up, he handed her one of the kerosene lamps. His dark eyes followed her as she made her way down the hall toward the bedroom. And then he turned the logs and poked up the fire before settling down again in his easy chair.

The tempting aroma of griddle cakes and coffee awakened Rowan the next morning. Following her nose to the kitchen, she found Brian cheerfully in charge of the cooking chores again.

"What time is it?" she asked.

He glanced at his watch. "Since you're on vacation, I let you sleep late. It's 8:30."

"That late!" Rowan mocked.

"Yeah. This is early to bed, early to rise country. Now quit complaining and set the table," he returned cheerfully.

Obediently Rowan reached down cups and plates from the overhead cabinets and found cutlery in the drawer.

Brian poured coffee and brought a stack of griddle cakes to the table, and they both dug in.

"What kind of syrup is this?" Rowan asked appreciatively after her first bite.

"Real maple."

"Are you trying to corrupt me? I'll never be able to eat the imitation stuff again," she retorted.

"Just displaying the advantages of country living," Brian answered lightly. "Speaking of which, I'm going to show you around the island after breakfast."

Pretending to turn her full attention back to her griddle cakes, Rowan watched him take a sip of coffee. He was at his disarming best this morning. But that did nothing to lessen her awareness of his physical presence.

It was a relief for Rowan to escape the confines of the cabin after breakfast.

"This island is something under a square mile," Brian told her as they wandered down a path through the pines and sumacs in back of the cabin. "But it's one of the larger ones around here."

"And just where is *here*?" she questioned.

He grinned. "I guess it can't do any harm to tell you. We're in the Thousand Islands, in the Saint Lawrence River, between Canada and the U.S. This particular island is in Canadian waters."

"The Thousand Islands?" Rowan persisted.

"Yes. That's what they're called, although there are really more than sixteen hundred of them. Some are just mounds of rock sticking out of the water. There's an old

95

Indian legend that long ago two warring gods stood on opposite sides of the river hurling great boulders at each other. The ones that fell short and landed in the water became the Thousand Islands."

Rowan grinned. "And do you believe it?"

"It's as good an explanation as any other," Brian countered, his dark eyes twinkling.

The trail led to another part of the shoreline, and as they approached the water Rowan saw a small boat speed past in the distance. Shading her eyes from the sun, she watched it disappear. Did many boats come this way? she wondered. Would there be any chance of rescue from a passerby?

"This island is a bit off the beaten track," Brian said, as if reading her thoughts. "That's why Larry likes it, because it's isolated."

"Oh."

"Don't sound so disappointed."

"Now you've got to admit—" Rowan began.

But Brian held up his hand. "Remember our truce," he cautioned.

Rowan bit her lip. If there was any way to get off of this rock in the St. Lawrence, she was going to find it. But in the meantime she'd have to watch her step.

"What can I do to convince you this is the vacation spot of North America?" Brian asked dramatically. Looking around at the ground for a moment, he stepped off the trail, leaned over, and picked a small spray of delicate blue bell-like flowers. With a mock bow he presented them to Rowan.

"What are they?" she asked, accepting the proffered blossoms.

"Harebell. And that gives me an idea." Rowan watched as he plucked another small sprig and then turned back to her. "Now hold still," he commanded. Placing one steadying hand on her cheek, he tucked the sprig into her hair, just above her ear.

Rowan dropped her gaze, willing herself not to tremble again at his touch.

But Brian broke the contact and stepped back quickly to survey his handiwork. "Charming." he pronounced.

Rowan felt a flush creeping into her cheeks.

"We'll have to decorate your hair with one of every flower in the woods," Brian declared.

CHAPTER SEVEN

During the days that followed, they explored their private paradise, Brian's easygoing, nonthreatening demeanor setting the tone. Randomly he led Rowan around the island, stopping often to comment upon the flora. During these treks, she learned to respect the breadth of his knowledge —and his obvious pleasure in the natural setting. This was a very different man from the Brian Turner she had met at a Washington cocktail party or the man who had discovered a stowaway on his boat. This was a man who could be a friend and companion. She already knew he could be a lover. In fact, only the knowledge that he wanted to be her lover marred the tranquil perfection of their first days together. In all their dealings the attraction between them hummed like unseen electricity. And at the end of each idyllic sunset the voltage seemed to build.

Late on the afternoon of the third day, after one of their botanical rambles, they rocked silently together on the cabin's rustic front porch. Rowan leaned back and closed her eyes. There were no traffic noises assaulting her ears. No babble of voices. No rock music blaring from radios. There was no sound but the rhythmic creak of her rocker treads against the worn porch boards and the occasional call of a bird high up in the pine trees.

Finally Brian broke the silence. "Want to help me catch dinner?"

"Sure."

"I'll get up the energy to move in a minute," he assured her.

"I'm ready when you are," Rowan replied.

Sighing heavily, Brian heaved himself out of his rocker and disappeared around the side of the cabin. When he returned, he was carrying two casting rods and a metal bait box. "Now you've got to get up," he challenged.

Rowan complied, and they started companionably off down the path toward the dock.

"Hope they're biting the way they were yesterday," he threw over his shoulder.

Rowan nodded, following him out onto the rough gray boards of the dock. But she had taken only a few steps when something sharp pierced her foot, and she gave a little cry of pain.

Brian dropped his fishing gear and turned around quickly. "What is it?" he asked urgently.

"My foot. I must have a splinter," Rowan explained, sitting down on the dock and pulling the sole of her right foot upward for inspection.

"Here, let me," he offered, sitting down beside her and grasping the foot with both hands. Running a thumb lightly over the surface, he felt gently for the injury. Rowan winced when he came in contact with the shred of gray wood. "It's a big one," Brian announced. "We'll have to get it out up at the cabin. Can't risk an infection out here in the middle of nowhere," he told her.

Grasping Rowan's hand, he helped her to her feet. "Don't put any pressure on the splinter," he cautioned. "Lean on me, and I'll help you back to the cabin."

Rowan wanted to draw away as he slipped one arm firmly around her waist, pulling the side of her body against his. "Put your arm around my shoulder," he commanded. "It'll be easier to walk."

"Really, I—" she began.

But he cut her off. "Don't be silly. The sooner we get it out, the better."

The walk back to the cabin was a slow one, with Rowan barely able to put any pressure on her right foot. All the way up the path she was acutely conscious of the man who supported her against the hard length of his body. She could feel his strong fingers pressing into her waist. And with every step she was forced to brush against his hip.

It was a relief when he finally helped her into an easy chair and retrieved the first-aid kit from the bathroom.

Pulling up a kitchen chair, he took her foot onto his lap and swabbed it with disinfectant. Then he produced a pair of tweezers from the medical kit. "If we're lucky, this will come out in one piece," he said, pulling firmly on the sliver of wood protruding from her flesh. But although he gave a strong, steady pull, the weathered wood came apart. "I'm afraid it's going to take a needle to get it out," Brian said apologetically.

Rowan nodded stoically, watching as he lit a match to sterilize the impromptu surgical tool.

"Tell me if I'm hurting you," he ordered.

But Rowan gritted her teeth. She tried to keep from wincing as she felt the steel point probing her foot. But she wasn't entirely successful.

"Want me to stop for a minute?" Brian questioned.

She shook her head. "No, just get it over with."

"Damn thing's pretty deep," Brian reported, working as gently as possible. Rowan closed her eyes, feeling the sweat break out on her upper lip. Teeth clamped together, she held herself rigid, as the jabs of pain came again.

"Got it," Brian finally announced with triumph. Rowan felt the cold sting of more antiseptic.

Opening her eyes she saw the look of concern on his face. "I didn't like having to hurt you," he said.

"You had to get it out," Rowan told him.

"Yes, but I should have thought about your running around here in bare feet, damnit. I shouldn't have taken you out on that dock."

Rowan shook her head. "It's not your fault really."

"But delicate little feet like these deserve to be taken care of," he murmured, running his finger gently along the tops of her toes.

Suddenly Rowan's heart began to beat violently in her chest. She was hotly aware that her foot was still resting in Brian's lap and that she could feel the texture of his hair-roughened thighs against her flesh. Bending her knee, she started to pull away, but Brian grasped her firmly by the ankle. "Let me put an adhesive bandage on to keep it clean." His fingers were infinitely gentle now as he pressed the bandage against her foot, stroking the adhesive to press it down. It was almost like a caress, and she closed her eyes again, leaning back against the sofa cushions, allowing herself to enjoy the intimate sensation.

She felt him let go reluctantly, and her eyes snapped open again.

"Tell you what," Brian said. "Let me look around and see if there's any kind of shoe here that won't fall off your foot."

Rowan swung her legs up on the sofa, listening to the sound of him rummaging in closets and drawers. When he reappeared, he was waving aloft a pair of cheap rubber beach thongs. "Try these on," he said, handing them to Rowan.

They were only a little too wide—but three inches too long. Holding up her foot, Rowan displayed the disparity.

"Not to worry," Brian told her, taking the sandals back. Pulling a scissors from the kitchen drawer, he unceremoniously cut off the back end of each sandal, rounding it to approximate the shape of Rowan's heel. "Not very elegant, but they ought to do," he announced. "Remind me that I owe Larry one pair of beach sandals."

Rowan stood up and slipped her good foot into one of the thongs. The fit was crude, but it would do. "As long as I stay on the straight and narrow," she observed.

Brian looked hurt. "Okay, then, I'll sweeten the deal.

I'll catch our fish dinner, and you relax—or whatever you want to do."

"You've got a deal."

When he was gone, Rowan hobbled back to her bedroom, putting as little weight as possible on her injured foot. Pulling off her T-shirt and cutoffs, she tossed them into a heap on the floor. Though Brian had offered her some of his own clothes earlier, his mystery friend, Larry, was a smaller man, and his things fit her better.

Remembering that the evening was likely to be chilly, Rowan dressed in a pair of jeans, the long legs of which she rolled thickly around her ankles, and cinched them tightly again at the waist. Another one of Larry's T-shirts completed her outfit. Although her foot hurt, she decided not to lie down.

Rowan didn't want Brian to take full responsibility for dinner. And so she hobbled gingerly into the kitchen and began looking through the larder and the boxes Brian had brought from the seaplane. All in all, there was quite a variety of food—everything from evaporated milk to canned and frozen vegetables, flour and semisweet baking chocolate. The latter gave her a good idea. On the back of the package were several recipes, and a quick search of the cupboards and refrigerator told her that the rest of the ingredients for one of them were also on hand.

By the time Brian returned from his fishing expedition, the cabin was fragrant with the aroma of baking brownies.

"What's this?" he exclaimed as he stepped through the front door.

Rowan grinned. "A little surprise. And you'll just have to wait to find out exactly what. So you might as well clean your fish."

He made a face. "You do know how to keep a fellow in suspense."

Rowan nodded her agreement. While Brian attended to

the fish she put together a rice pilaf and set it on the burner to simmer.

Forty minutes later they sat down again to another feast. This time Brian had landed a good size pike, which went splendidly with the rice and the broccoli Rowan had also cooked. And there was another bottle of excellent wine.

"Just what is your arrangement with Larry about the food?" Rowan asked as she reached for her brimming glass.

Brian shook his head. "That's not something you have to worry about." Although the words were casually spoken, their intent came through loud and clear to Rowan. The subject of his arrangements with their absent host was off limits. And if she pressed the matter, the rapprochement they had worked out over the last few days might be jeopardized.

Liking the easy relationship they had been able to establish, she quickly changed the subject. "For some perverse reason all this food reminds me of the time Bill's star reporter, Wally Harding, went off to do a story on some religious cult living on a farm in West Virginia. They invited him to stay with them for a week or so—sharing their communal household, as it were. They made him chop wood and scrub floors—so he'd understand the spiritual meaning of work. He had to live on their macrobiotic diet—you know, almost nothing but brown rice. He ended up losing ten pounds. And they had the nerve to send him a bill for his food."

Brian chuckled. "Sounds like he asked for it."

"Well, Wally will do anything to get a story. Once, before he came to work for Bill, he dressed up like a maid so he could get into Natalie Wood's hotel room. She was taking a bath at the time and had him scrub her back."

Brian almost choked on the sip of wine he had just taken. "You're kidding," he gasped.

Rowan grinned mischievously. "Actually, he may have been exaggerating."

"So it's not just your brother who taught you everything you know," her dinner companion observed. "You're following in Wally's footsteps too."

The remark brought Rowan up short. Although she did admire her colleague's ability to get a story, she had always considered him a bit brash and uncouth. The idea that Brian would compare the two of them was actually quite unsettling—and unflattering, she admitted. And yet Brian didn't really know Wally, she assured herself. He only knew what she had just told him.

To her surprise she found that Brian had sensed her mood and wanted to salve her feelings. "But I'll bet you could give old Wally cooking lessons any day," he observed. "That pilaf was terrific. What's your mystery dessert?"

"Brownies," she replied, glad that he was willing to drop his previous line of speculation so easily.

"How did you know I have a weakness for chocolate?" he asked now.

Rowan let herself respond to his light mood. "Your provisions were a dead giveaway." Pushing back her chair, she crossed to the kitchen counter and began arranging the brownies on a plate. Standing at the counter she was aware that the foot she had injured that afternoon hardly bothered her any more.

"Let's take the brownies into the living room," Brian suggested, pushing back his own chair. Rowan watched him cross to the fireplace and begin to stack up the logs as he had the previous evening. Soon the dry wood was alight with tongues of flame. "Shouldn't we do the dishes first?" Rowan asked, but Brian shook his head. Moving to the kitchen, he turned down the kerosene lamps, so that the room's main illumination now came from the fireplace.

"With the lights down low, you can pretend they're not there," he suggested with a great show of logic.

Rowan shook her head. "You'll be sorry tomorrow morning."

"We'll worry about it tomorrow, then," he replied, making his way back to one of the wing chairs facing the fire and reaching for a brownie from the plate Rowan had set on the coffee table. "Umm," he grunted approvingly.

Rowan took one of the rich chocolate squares and followed suit. "You're right," she agreed. "They are good."

Brian chuckled. "That's what I like in a woman—modesty."

"You mean honesty," she corrected, leaning back in her own chair. The darkened room was having a strange effect on Rowan. She could not see Brian's face and knew he must not be able to see hers either. Somehow the lack of visual contact made her feel separate and protected, as though she were somehow safe in the shadows.

They sat in silence for several moments.

"If you're in an honest mood, will you answer a serious question?" Brian suddenly asked, the timbre of his voice deepening oddly.

"It depends," she answered, trying to keep her tone light.

"Have you ever been in love?"

If she had been able to see Brian, she most probably would not have answered. But, enveloped in her cocoon of darkness, she heard herself answering, "Yes. I was."

"Was?"

"It's all over now."

"Want to tell me what happened?" he prompted gently.

And Rowan realized that she did. Haltingly at first, and then with more assurance, she began to tell him about Charles Fogel, the man she had thought she wanted to marry until she had learned of his involvement in the GSA contract-peddling scheme.

Brian let her talk without interruption, only punctuating her monologue with an occasional "uh-huh." And she was so wound up in her story that she didn't hear the tone of his laconic responses become harsher.

When at last she had spun out the whole story, she felt immensely better, as though she had been holding some guilty secret inside and had finally let it go.

With a start she heard the scrape of a chair from the other side of the room. And in the flickering light from the fire she was suddenly aware of movement. Then Brian was standing in front of her, pulling her to her feet with strong, viselike hands. In the dark she felt his grip tighten on her shoulders. Alarmed, she tried to twist away, but he held her fast.

"So, you've been punishing me for Charles Fogel all this time," he rasped. "Well, I'm not not like him, whatever you may think."

"What—what do you mean?" she quavered in the darkness.

"I mean, you've been assuming that because Charles was involved in something crooked, I am too. Well, I won't be mistaken for another man. Before the evening's over, you're going to be very aware that you're with Brian Turner, not Charles Fogel." And with that his lips descended to take possession of hers while his hands slipped from her shoulders to her back and hips. Rowan felt her body pulled firmly against the length of Brian's. There was no doubt in her mind what man held her in his arms. All the sexual tension that had been smoldering between the two of them suddenly came crackling to life. Without conscious thought Rowan found her mouth opening to the insistent exploration of Brian's tongue while her body molded itself to the contours of his. She felt a sensual heat kindle in her abdomen and spread downward to her loins as Brian's hands caressed her hips and then slid around to cup her buttocks and pull her even closer against him.

It was his sigh of male satisfaction that brought Rowan up short. What was she allowing to happen? If she didn't break away from Brian now, there would be no stopping him—and no stopping herself either.

Confident of his power over her, Brian no longer held her as though she might try to free herself from his grasp. Instead, his hands had begun a butterfly-light caressing of her body. The raw force of her reaction was both exciting and frightening. Suddenly overwhelmed and confused, Rowan took Brian by surprise. Pulling away quickly, she fled across the room and out the door of the cabin.

But once outside, she hesitated. There had been no thought of a plan in her mind when she had broken away, only her fear of her overwhelming reaction to this man. Yet, as she stood, frustrated and uncertain in the darkness, she began to ask herself why she had run from Brian, when in truth she wanted nothing more than to make love with him. How could she counter the magnetic pull that drew them together. And did she even want to?

The night was quite black as only a night in the wilds can be. Clouds had obscured the moon, and the few stars gave no real light.

Despite her daytime rambles with Brian, Rowan did not know the island well. The only trail she could be sure of now was the main one that led to the dock. But there was no conscious plan in her mind, only confused self-doubts.

Ahead of her Rowan could now see the water glistening faintly beyond the trees. But she never reached the edge of the pines. On feet silent as an Indian brave's tracking a deer, Brian was suddenly at her side, his broad hand on her shoulder. The unexpected contact made Rowan jump, a muffled "oh" of surprise escaping from her lips. But her startled reaction had no effect on her determined pursuer. This time, to Rowan's sudden delight and relief, he was not about to let his quarry escape. With one fluid motion he swung her up into his sinewy arms and pulled her body against his broad chest. And then he was striding with her back toward the open cabin door, just visible in the glow from the fireplace.

She knew now that any thought of escape had been folly. There was no escaping the bond between them. What was going to happen had been inevitable from the moment she'd set eyes on him at April Coster's party.

As he crossed the cabin's threshold she buried her face against his neck. "What do you do with your female captives?" she whispered, her heart beginning to hammer in her throat.

"I ravish them," he rumbled deep in his chest as he headed down the hall toward the bedrooms.

In the darkness Rowan did not know which room he had chosen as she felt herself being lowered gently onto a broad bed.

This time Brian was taking no chances on her escape. Holding her slender wrists easily in one of his hands, he pulled her arms above her head, rolled her over onto her side, and stretched the length of his hard body beside hers. As Rowan felt the contact of his muscular chest against her breasts and his lithe hips against hers, her breath quickened. She knew that any real struggle on her part would release his grip. There was no need for him to hold her fast. She was truly his captive now, not through physical restraint but through her own overwhelming desire. And yet, somehow, the circlet of his flesh around her wrists was an added stimulus to that desire.

His face was only inches from her own, and she felt his warm breath mingle with hers.

"Brian," she sighed, the word suffused with all the pent-up longing she had tried for so long to deny.

She was so closely attuned to him that when she felt his fingertips on her face, delicately tracing the plane of her cheek and the line of her jaw, an ecstatic shiver ran through her body. And she knew he could feel her strong response to the light caress. He understood finally that she was incapable of leaving him tonight. Releasing her wrists, his right hand tangled itself possessively in her luxuriant curls while his left began a languorous caress of her shoulders and back. His lips found the pulse point at the base of her neck, lingering there for several heartbeats. And then he lifted his head to study her face. His eyes were dark forest pools, still and deep. And Rowan felt as though she might drown in their bottomless depths.

In wonder her own hands lowered themselves to Brian's face and neck, finding tactile gratification in the feel of his skin. Then her lips boldly sought his. If Brian was surprised at her eager aggressiveness, he gave no sign. She felt as much as heard his groan of pleasure as her impudent tongue began to explore the delicious recesses of his mouth. And her satisfaction at his response was a spur to her own desire.

Her lips left his to follow the path over his face and neck that her fingers had taken only moments before. The male aroma of his body was as much a sensual delight as the feel of his skin against her face.

"Rowan," she heard him whisper, his breath warm against her ear, "why did you run from me?"

"I was afraid," she admitted in a small voice.

"And now?"

"Now there's only one thing that matters."

"Yes," he agreed.

The clouds had rolled away from the face of the moon, and a silvery radiance was streaming in through the uncurtained window. Rowan watched as Brian gently pulled her to a sitting position on the bed. And then his hands found the edge of her T-shirt. Raising her arms above her head, she made it easy for him to remove the outsize garment. In a moment her bra had followed it to the rug beside the bed.

Naked to the waist, she faced him then. And the dark passion she saw in his eyes and play of strong emotion across his chiseled features made her nipples harden as though from a physical embrace.

"My God, you're beautiful," he breathed.

When his hands came up to cup and caress her breasts,

she gave a soft little moan of pleasure. And when his fingertips found her hardened nipples, the pleasure intensified, turning the very blood in her veins to liquid fire.

He bent his head to bury his face in the soft valley between her breasts. And then he turned to take her right nipple in his mouth, teasing it with his lips and tongue before flexing his cheeks to suck the sweetness of her. Unconsciously Rowan brought her hands up to cradle his head, her body swaying slightly.

"Oh, Brian," she murmured. "That feels so good, so incredibly good . . ."

After a long moment he lifted his face to smile down at her. "For me too," he acknowledged, his voice rough with passion.

She felt his hands then on the rope belt at her waist and couldn't suppress a wicked giggle. "Shall I turn around so you'll be able to undo the square knot?" she teased.

"Oh, by all means," he agreed, stretching her out on her side in the bed and lying down in back of her with his chest pressed tightly against her shoulder blades. Reaching around her body, as he had done once before, he made swift work of the knot and then slid her jeans and silky panties down her legs and over her ankles.

Rowan expected him to turn her around then. But he held her prisoner against the length of his taut body, her back and hips pressed firmly against him.

This position gave him free access to her most sensitive places. And he took full advantage of it. With his free hand he began slowly to caress her body, paying court again to her breasts and then moving downward to her hips and thighs. His touch on her skin brought her to throbbing arousal. And when his fingers moved silkily between her legs to find the very heart of her femininity, she arched her back against him and moaned. She felt his lips raining fiery little kisses on the back of her neck, the lobes of her ears, the tops of her shoulders. And she want-

110

ed desperately to turn and face him. But the heat spreading through her body had turned her bones to wax.

Brian shifted his hold so that one leg and shoulder held her fast. Now with both hands free, he began a devastatingly sensual assault on her body. One hand began to tantalize her breasts, while at the same time his fingers slid high up between her legs, to stroke and fondle the part of her that most wanted his attention. For Rowan, the exquisite pleasure of that double caress was almost too much to bear.

"Please, Brian," she gasped.

"Please what?" It was his turn to tease now.

"My God, let me turn around."

She hadn't known that he too was at the limit of his endurance. Swiftly he pivoted her toward him, lowering his lips to drink in the sweetness of her mouth like a thirsty man at an oasis.

In the next instant she felt him move away, and her eyes snapped open in surprise before she realized that he was only removing his clothing.

This time when he pulled her against the length of his body, there was no barrier to their intimacy. Neither could get enough of the other now. Her fingers twined in the rough hair of his chest, while her lips sought his flat male nipples. His hands caressed her face and then moved lower to begin a new exploration of her quivering body.

"I want you so much," she heard him whisper in her ear. And it was true for her as well. There was a deep, hollow ache inside her, an ache which only Brian Turner could assuage.

Desire made her bold. "Don't make me wait," she implored. And he was quick to comply. With one swift motion he entered her. It took only a moment for them to find the natural rhythm of their mutual pleasure. Rowan marveled at the perfect unity of their climb to the brink of rapture, neither withholding anything from the other. For her, in that moment out of time, the barrier which had

111

separated them no longer mattered or even existed. There was only an equal giving and taking of wondrous joy. Each urged the other upward toward the heights of ecstasy until together they tumbled over the edge of passionate fulfillment.

Afterwards Brian drew Rowan tightly into the circle of his arms. Neither of them spoke, for words seemed out of place now. But as he nuzzled her hair with his lips Brian marveled at the experience they had just shared. He had brought her to this island bent on mere seduction—a pleasant interlude and no more. But what they had just experienced was no mere interlude. It had been a strong and powerful fusion, not just of their bodies but of their very souls.

The night Rowan's tape recorder had malfunctioned, and again when she had hidden herself on his boat, he had thought he knew what kind of woman she was. But that was impossible to believe now. Away from the influence of Bill Emory and his unholy crew, she was something quite different. He knew now she was a woman to cherish —the kind of woman he had been looking for all his life. And more than that, she was the woman with whom he wanted to share the rest of his life.

CHAPTER EIGHT

Rowan awoke to feel pale fingers of gray light touching her lids. With a jolt she came fully conscious to realize she was naked and covered only by a sheet. At that moment she felt the bed creak and shift as someone heavy next to her stirred and then rolled over. Hot, betraying color surged up in her face, and her eyes widened. Brian was next to her, the powerful line of his back sculpted in shadow by the pale light of dawn.

As she stared like one hypnotized at the short, fine hairs marking his spine a prickle of sexual awareness made her nipples stiffen, and she remembered with shattering clarity all that had occurred the night before.

Brian's lovemaking had seemed so right, so exquisitely satisfying then. But now, as she lay in bed next to him, thinking over her plight in the thin gray light of morning, she was beset by doubts and uncertainties. Moodily she cast another look at his relaxed, sleeping body and then averted her face and bit her lip. This wouldn't be the first time her heart had ruled her head. She had completely misjudged Charles Fogel and fallen in love with a handsome face that masked a very unhandsome person. And now, despite the warnings from Bill, despite her knowledge that Brian might be both dangerous and thoroughly unscrupulous, she'd tumbled headlong into that emotional maelstrom again. She remembered only too clearly her strong reaction the moment she'd set eyes on him that fateful night of their first meeting. But that had been

113

nothing to the way she'd finally surrendered to his impassioned lovemaking last night.

It had been wonderful, she acknowledged, but it had also been foolish of her. Rowan almost groaned aloud as she reviewed her situation. Alone and unprotected, she was on an isolated island with a man she'd been assigned to investigate. Well, she'd investigated him all right. By now she knew him almost as well as he must know every nook and cranny of her. His explorations had been thorough last night. Her loins began to glow with remembered fire as she recalled the mindless excitement his hands and mouth had generated as they caressed her flesh, molding her to his will like an artist shaping compliant clay.

At that moment Brian stirred and rolled over. Her head turned to survey the relaxed lines of his face. Was she falling in love with him? she asked herself, seriously unnerved. How else could she explain her behavior last night? It was anything but typical. A cold shiver doused all the sexual awareness she had been feeling. Brian Turner was not a safe man to love. Aside from his doubtful ethics, he was a well-known charmer with a string of beautiful socialites at his beck and call. What could she offer him but an insignificantly amusing bit of dalliance?

Rowan surveyed his handsome features with growing wariness. He was sleeping like a baby, a satisfied smile curling his shapely mouth. No wonder he looked so satisfied; he had exposed her weakness for him last night and made her behave like a besotted idiot. He had whispered sweet words in her ear, and she had melted like sugar. But he had said nothing of love itself. And why should he bother to mention that tender emotion? Rowan asked herself starkly. She had angered him at first. But he had put her in her place—his bed. They said that women were the weaker sex. She had refused to accept that before, but she had to wonder now if it wasn't true—at least in her own case.

At that moment Rowan's bleak gaze dropped onto the tumbled pile of clothes next to the bed. Brian's jeans were lying where they had fallen the night before. A bit of white cloth showed where one of the pocket linings had been pulled out. From it a curved bar of silver-colored metal glinted in the pale sunlight that was beginning to spill over the braided rug. Rowan's eyes narrowed as she stared at the turned-out pocket. Then her whole body went tense under the sheets as she realized what was glinting and beckoning at her. It was a key ring. Would one of its keys unlock the radio shed she'd discovered earlier?

Her skin went cold, and she began to tremble. If she could take the keys and slip out of the room unnoticed, she might be able to send a distress call. Doing that very thing had been in her mind earlier, and now the opportunity had presented itself. Did she want to take it? Her head turned again, and she stared into Brian's unconscious face as though it might answer the questions racing through her brain. But his relaxed features offered no clues to his true self or his real feelings toward her. It was the face of a sinfully handsome man who'd had his way with her last night. He rolled away again. The unconscious movement seemed to answer her fearful queries. If she didn't seize this chance for rescue and he turned out to be the opportunist Bill took him for, she would curse herself for a gullible fool the rest of her days.

Stealthily Rowan slid from the bed and reached into Brian's open pocket, clamping her fist firmly around the keys inside so they wouldn't jingle as she drew them out. Then she grabbed her own clothes from the floor and silently slipped out of the room. To avoid any further recriminations, she pulled her clothes on quickly in the living room and then tiptoed out onto the porch. It was very early. Pink streaks were just beginning to wash the lightening sky. The grass was soaked with dew, and it wet her shoeless feet as she padded softly toward the shoreline and the route she had taken the first morning when she'd accidentally come across the locked shed. It was chilly and Rowan shivered with only her thin T-shirt for protection. But she did not slacken her pace. Now that she'd decided to go ahead with this thing, she was determined to get it over as quickly as possible.

When she rounded the next bend, the antenna swung into view, a silvery filament against the streaky sky. Taking a deep breath, Rowan plunged into the uphill scrub that would lead her to it. Her slim brown legs ate up the distance, and within minutes she had reached the hilltop clearing she'd investigated earlier. The hut was still there, of course. Only now it seemed less mysteriously inviting and more threatening. Extracting Brian's keys from her pocket, she tried them one by one on the unyielding lock that had defied all her efforts before. The first three didn't fit, and she sighed with unthinking relief as she searched out the fourth and inserted it in the lock. If none of the keys was right, then the decision was taken out of her hands. She would have done all she could do. But the last one slid in like silk, and when she automatically turned the knob, the door swung open. Inside, on a table, was a radio in a metal cabinet the size of a small stereo. It was a model she was familiar with. The die was cast—there could be no excuse now for not going through with what she planned.

The generator outside the hut started up easily. The little motor was noisy, but surely, she told herself, Brian would not hear it at this distance. Once inside the shed and seated in front of the radio, she had no trouble turning it on and tuning to a ten-meter frequency. While she went through these operations, she debated whether to send out a distress call or try finding a conversation to interrupt. At this hour of the morning on the east coast she would be lucky to discover people talking. But fate seemed determined to make the call a success. She found a conversation immediately. Two men were discussing the relative merits of various Canadian and U.S. hockey teams. But they broke off at once when she cut in with her plea for help.

In the past few days her sleuthing and careful questions had pieced together a fair amount of information about the island and its owner. Since she didn't want the police brought in on the matter, she left out any mention of kidnaping. Instead she implied that Bill was her father and that she had borrowed his boat and run aground on Larry's island. She gave her approximate location and asked that Bill be informed, as he was undoubtedly worried about her. But the signal began to fade toward the end of her message. And though she tried to bring the two men back in, she couldn't be sure that she'd gotten enough information across to effect a rescue. Should she try again? But that was risky. Brian might wake up, miss her, and miss his keys as well. What would come of her impulsive action? she wondered as she carefully locked the door to the radio shack and started back down the hill. Now that the deed was actually done and she no longer had a surge of adrenaline to spur her on, she experienced a sinking sensation. Should she really have done this? Last night had been a beautiful experience, and now it was spoiled. Already she was beginning to feel she'd made a mistake.

That feeling grew stronger when she returned to the bedroom she'd shared with Brian and quietly returned the keys to his pocket. He was still sleeping peacefully, his strong, regular features relaxed in the brighter light dancing over the bed. Though he hadn't awakened, there were signs he had missed her in her absence. His naked arm was thrown out, the hand curled loosely around the pillow where her head had rested an hour earlier. The gesture was like a reproach. Disquieted by it and oddly moved, Rowan turned away with a hollow feeling. What had she done? Brian had come to mean more to her in the last few days than even she could fully comprehend. And now she had betrayed him.

Outside on the porch she sank into a sturdy redwood

rocker. At the other end of the packed dirt path the sun was beginning to glint on the water, heralding a perfect high-summer day. Rowan stared blankly at its promise, her eyes shimmering with the same shade of deep translucent blue while she wrestled with the question of her real feelings for Brian Turner.

An hour later he found her curled up there like an unhappy child. As he emerged from the house, wearing jeans and an old sweatshirt cut off in ragged lines at the sleeves, a deep frown furrowed his brow and his eyebrows formed a straight line over his deep-set eyes. But his troubled expression cleared instantly when he spied the woman who'd become his lover. She was rocking slowly and staring morosely out at the sparkling river as though it held some dark secret.

"So there you are!" he called out. "I missed you when I woke up. Why'd you get up so early? From now on I want to wake up and find you there beside me."

Though Rowan was powerfully aware of him, she didn't turn her head to answer his lightheartedly suggestive greeting. Her own heart was anything but light, and she was not in the right frame of mind to reply to remarks like that. Sensing her changed mood, Brian's frown reappeared and he moved forward quickly to place a hand on Rowan's unruly curls. Instead of responding, she averted her face, and all he could see of her expression was her pale, set mouth and the tears that glittered in her lowered eyelashes.

"Rowan," he said deeply, "what's wrong?" When she didn't answer, he dropped down on one knee beside the rocker. Cupping her chin gently, he turned her face toward his. "Rowan, don't do this. What's the problem?"

Her sapphire gaze flickered and dropped before his probing inspection. "Nothing," she mumbled unconvincingly.

Brian's fingers tightened in reaction. "Don't give me

that! It's last night, isn't it? You're upset about what happened between us."

Defensively she wrapped her arms tighter about her chest while she jerked her chin free from his grasp. "Last night was a mistake!" she choked out, horrified by the desperate ring of her voice. But it was true, she thought miserably. From the first, everything that had happened between her and Brian had been a mistake!

But he wasn't accepting that. Slowly he shook his head. "The way you responded to me was so right, so perfect," he countered, his voice deep and husky with emotion. "There was no mistake about last night. It was the most fantastic thing that ever happened to me. But it isn't just sex, Rowan. There's more to it than that. There's something very special between us. Let's give it a chance."

Rowan blinked and stared at him in shock. Was he telling the truth? Their lovemaking had been wonderful. And it had been much more than a mere physical thing for her. Had it meant as much to him? But that seemed so unlikely. He was an experienced man and undoubtedly had a complicated love life. How could their experience together have been earthshaking for him? And if it had, that would make her radio call this morning downright despicable. Damned by every possibility that faced her, she had to believe that for him she was only one more night's entertainment in a long string of affairs. Because, if that wasn't true, if he really did care for her, then she had just destroyed her chance at happiness.

When Rowan shook her head to emphasize her disbelief, Brian smiled shrewdly into her doubting eyes and stroked a firm finger down the soft line of her cheek. Though her responsive skin burned at his touch, she managed to maintain her coolly rebellious demeanor.

"You'll see," he promised warmly. "Maybe I can't convince you with words, but when we make love again, you'll see how special things are between us. You won't be able to deny the truth then."

Rowan's reaction was not what he'd been looking for. Her azure eyes flashed with anger. "We aren't going to make love again," she said tightly. "And if you cared anything for me, you'd let me go right now. You wouldn't keep me a prisoner here with you."

Brian rocked back on his heels and studied her impassive face. He guessed he could understand why she was behaving this way. Things had happened between them in a topsy-turvy fashion. She had started out suspecting him of evil deeds, and maybe she was still suspicious of his motives. But surely last night should have made clear his real feelings for her, he reasoned. There was something very special between them. He had felt it when they first met, and now he knew it in his bones and his blood. Right now Rowan was upset, but in her heart she must realize the truth. Before the day was over they would be lovers again, he reassured himself, and then she wouldn't be able to deny that they were made to be part of each other.

"Look, I know I was wrong to force you into staying here with me," he conceded gently. "But it's done, and I can't honestly say I'm sorry, because in the long run I believe it's going to be the best thing for both of us. I've been in touch with my lawyer, and he thinks that in a few days I'll be vindicated. What's more, you needed to get away from that rat race." He smiled, his face suffused with charm. "Admit it, Rowan, Larry's island isn't so bad."

She put her lips together and gave him a dry look. Teasingly he reached out a lazy hand and pulled one of her curls. "Have you had any breakfast?"

She shook her head, and he grinned down at her knowingly, the corners of his mouth lifting with amusement. "That explains why you're so grouchy. Just to show what a genial jailer I really am, I'm going to fix a great breakfast for the two of us."

In one lithe movement he was on his feet and striding lightly toward the cabin's screen door. From her hunched position in the rocker Rowan watched him secretly through the silken curtain of her lashes. Her eyes dwelt on the firm, rounded contours of his buttocks in the tight-fitting jeans. Everything about him attracted her, she thought with despair. Even with his back to her, his latent male sexuality made her body vibrate sympathetically.

Brian was as good as his word. Minutes after he'd disappeared, the tantalizing aroma of fresh-brewed coffee and frying bacon wafted out to Rowan's quivering nostrils. And all at once she realized how ravenous she was. Her stomach was an empty, protesting pit crying out for food! At last she uncoiled herself, got up from the rocker, and moved toward the intoxicating aroma. Brian was in the kitchen. Sunlight flooded the cheerful room, and his black hair glinted almost iridescent in the brilliant light. He glanced at her over his shoulder, his expression relaxed and welcoming.

"Can I do anything to help?" she asked. Perhaps their relationship could be put back on a casual footing, she told herself, not believing it even as she formulated the thought.

"Thanks," he said, dishing scrambled eggs into a shallow bowl. "You can fill our cups with coffee."

The table, she observed, had been cleared of last night's dishes and was already set. Glasses of golden juice stood next to each plate, and a platter held strips of crisp bacon and toasted English muffins. Rowan poured coffee while Brian sat down and sipped his juice, his eyes wandering in open appreciation over her bare arms and legs.

"A beautiful morning," he observed, glancing at the window. "What would you like to do?"

Her gaze followed his. "Yes," she agreed, sliding onto her chair and pouring milk into her coffee until it was a creamy shade of beige. "I don't know. Surely by now you've shown me every wild flower on the island."

Brian grinned and picked up half a muffin. "Not every one. There's still a lot to see." He took a bite and chewed thoughtfully. "Are my botany lessons boring you? Because if they are, we could switch over to biology and spend the day in bed. I'd vote for that anyway."

Rowan choked on her eggs and gave him a pointed look. "I told you how I feel about that. If it's a choice between botany and biology, I'll go with the trees and flowers and forget the birds and bees."

Brian made a production of looking crestfallen but then began once more to cheerfully wolf down his eggs and bacon. "I have a suggestion," he offered between mouthfuls. "There's one special spot I haven't shown you yet. It's a spring-fed pool in the interior of the island. It's a pretty place and crystal clear. I'll even promise not to bother you if you want to try skinnydipping there."

"You promised that before," Rowan muttered, unconvinced, as she buttered a crisp muffin for herself.

Brian continued chewing with obvious relish and then washed down his mouthful of eggs with coffee. "This time it's Scout's Honor," he informed her, his features carefully composed. "I promise not to peek." And then his solemn demeanor slid into an outrageous leer. "I'll just use my imagination and my very good memory for detail."

Rowan tossed her buttered English muffin at him and then dissolved into helpless laughter. How could she keep this man at arm's length? she asked herself, wiping teary eyes with the corner of a paper napkin. He ducked right under her guard every time. He seemed able to sense all her moods and understand her vulnerabilities—almost as if they were an old married couple who'd known each other for years. The thought brought her up short and her expression sobered. What was she doing imagining them married? A relationship like that between her and Brian Turner was impossible. For her own sake, she'd better keep that clearly in mind.

As he took note of the expressions chasing themselves across her mobile face Brian scrutinized her quizzically. But he said nothing, and the rest of the meal was finished in relative silence. Brian completed his breakfast and leaned back, drinking a second cup of coffee and watching the woman opposite him with dark, intent eyes.

"We'll clean up here and then pack a picnic lunch," he suggested.

"All right," she agreed. Anything to break up the warm feeling of intimacy that had settled over them once again. Surely a long walk out in the open would be safe enough.

But there was nothing safe about Brian's company, she discovered. As they strolled along a wooded path later that morning her tingling awareness of his vital male body only strengthened. Their hips and legs always seemed to be brushing as they walked side by side. And on the frequent occasions when he stopped to point out an unusual bird or plant, his arm would drop naturally around her shoulder or wrap itself around her waist while the sinewy bronze fingers splayed themselves possessively along the feminine curve of her hip. He was doing it deliberately, she realized, as she forced herself again and again to break away from these disturbing contacts. In a hundred different ways he was holding out to her a sensual invitation that she was finding increasingly difficult to resist. Her whole being yearned to mold itself against him and lose herself in his arms. Her weak flesh ached for that union.

Later that morning she turned the problem over in her restless mind while she floated on her back in the crystal pool Brian had described. Her face was turned up to the sky, where the sun looked back like a glittering golden eye, and only an occasional puffy white cloud flawed the perfect azure of the heavens. Everything about this setting was perfect, her wayward mind mused: the limpid pool, the enclosing green pines which gave it absolute privacy. It was the ideal spot for a lovers' tryst, and though Brian, true to his word, had left her alone to swim, part of her wished he hadn't been such a gentleman. If he came back now, shed his clothes, and joined her in the water, she guessed they would make love. Just the thought of it made her skin feel so hot that she wondered, with amused disgust at her own traitorous imagination, why the water didn't steam and bubble around her.

When Brian returned, he found her dressed and lying on her stomach on a flat ledge with her hair spread around her head in damp curls.

"Have a good swim?" he asked pleasantly.

"Yes," she muttered, a betraying flush beginning to creep up her cheeks as she remembered her erotic fancies in the water. Conjecturing that she'd had too much sun, Brian solicitously dropped a straw hat over her head to protect her delicate skin.

"How about lunch?" he inquired equably, kneeling to rummage in the backpack he'd brought with him.

"All right," she agreed, sitting up and folding her legs under her. She was glad of the hat. Its shadow allowed her to study him from a protected vantage point. As he bent over the pack, lifting out bread, cold meat, eggs, and tomatoes, her eyes lingered on the muscles of his arms and broad back, and the way his crisp hair curled over the top of his collar. When he looked her way, she hastily turned her head and commented with false enthusiasm on the scenery.

"I'm glad you suggested this place. It's wonderful."

"Yes," he agreed. "But you add a lot to it." He shot her a wicked look. "I bet you made a delectable water nymph. While you were swimming I was lying under a tree fantasizing about how it would be to surprise you in the water. I wanted to swim up under you and kiss you all over."

Once more Rowan looked away, feeling her cheeks redden. While she had been swimming they had both been imagining the same delicious things.

When lunch was finished and the food cleared away, Rowan began to yawn.

"We could both use a nap," Brian suggested, unfolding the blanket he'd brought and spreading it in the shade at the foot of the rock where they had picnicked. Rowan eyed the blanket uncertainly. There wasn't much room on

124

it. How would she get to sleep so close to Brian's body? But it would look silly now to make a fuss about it.

Nevertheless, when he was stretched out next to her, she found herself lying stiffly on the blanket and very much awake. Somewhere a bird twittered. Otherwise there was only the faint slap of water and his regular breathing breaking the forest stillness. As she gradually became aware that he was asleep Rowan relaxed and turned her head to study with fascination his strong profile and the thick strands of black hair falling across his forehead. Her eyes drifted lower to the powerful lines of his chest under the blue chambray shirt, and then lower still to the masculinity revealed by his close-fitting jeans. The sight of him like this was an aphrodisiac, and she closed her eyes to ward off the arrant longings it provoked. She must have fallen asleep then, because the next thing she knew an insect was crawling annoyingly along the line of her eyebrows. She flapped at it with a languid hand, but what she encountered was a leaf wielded by a set of sinewy masculine fingers. She opened her drowsy eyes to absorb the dark, laughing gleam of Brian's.

"What—what are you doing?" she murmured fuzzily.

"I'm waking you up before you dump me into the water."

Her hazy blue eyes opened wide at that. It was true, she realized with a small gasp. In her sleep she had wrapped herself around him like a limpet. His head was so close to hers that his breath felt warm against her lips and their legs were entwined.

"I'm sorry."

"Don't be. I like it," he answered huskily as his mouth began to lower to hers.

"Brian, no," she breathed weakly.

"Rowan, yes," he returned with absolute conviction. And then his lips began to brush hers seductively while his hand stroked possessively down the length of her body from breast to thigh. "You're mine," he whispered sternly in her ear. "My woman. And I'm going to claim you here and now for all the birds and bees to see and take note."

She would have laughed, but he gave her no chance. Hungrily his mouth was on hers again, his tongue plundering its sweetness like a ravenous bear. Part of her bemused brain told her to refuse, that allowing this to happen again was insanity. But another part, louder and more insistent, clamored that the delight Brian offered was too rare and precious not to seize. Both of her hands buried themselves in his thick hair, luxuriating in the vital feel of it. And all the while his kiss went on, draining her of any lingering remnants of doubt, infusing her with a heated urgency that matched his.

When Brian finally lifted his head, he looked searchingly into the bottomless depths of her eyes, so like the water surrounding them. "You see," he whispered huskily.

"Yes," Rowan admitted, her steamy blue gaze never leaving his. "Yes, I see."

Slowly, caressingly, Brian undid the buttons of her shirt and opened it. She had not bothered to wear her bra, and so her rounded breasts offered themselves to his sensuous inspection without hindrance.

"So sweet," he murmured, his brown fingers circling them with delicate precision. She shivered at the delicious contact. Once again, his dark head lowered so that he could take one soft peak in his mouth, by turns sucking and tracing an erotic pattern with his deft tongue.

As quickening heat flamed down her body, Rowan moaned and her hands went eagerly to his shirt. She pulled it free of his waistband so that her fingers could track their own fiery path along the strong ridge of his backbone, kneading and massaging the muscles she found there. In response, she felt the hard thrust of Brian's urgent arousal pressing through the clothing they both still wore.

His mouth left her breasts, and he levered himself up on

126

one elbow to look at her again. With a sense of power, she noted that his face was flushed and he was breathing hard.

"I want you in the water, the way I imagined it."

Rowan stared at him confusedly. "What? We'll drown."

His hand pressed against her lips. "Trust me." Turning, he unsnapped her cutoffs and slipped them from her hips and legs along with her panties. Dropping, quick, hungry kisses on the skin of her stomach, pelvis, and thighs, he pulled her to a sitting position and removed her shirt so that she was completely naked in the warm afternoon sunlight. In the next moment he had divested himself of his own clothing, making the startling extent of his eagerness fully visible.

"Brian," she gasped as he knelt to pick her up easily and then slid off the edge of the rock with her still in his arms. The water was cool against her skin so that she shivered and gave a small shriek. But the shiver had more to do with delight than anything else. The liquid core of her femininity was still burning with anticipation.

As Brian found his feet on the bottom, the water rose up to his shoulders so that Rowan could not stand up. She was helpless in his knowing hands now, and he set about taking full advantage of her dependency. Laughing with masculine triumph into her flushed features, he lifted her above his head so that he could bury his face in her water-jeweled breasts. As he took each one in his mouth, Rowan clenched her hands around his bronzed shoulders and threw back her head, looking up into the blue dome of the sky and savoring the hot, delightful sensations running riot through the center of her charged body.

Then, with an athlete's agility, Brian lifted her higher so that he could rain delicate kisses under her breasts and down to the soft pit of her stomach, nuzzling the responsive flesh there while she gasped and wriggled.

But his need to feel her body pressed against his once again asserted itself. "Quite an active little mermaid I've got here," he whispered in her ear as he lowered her close against the hard length of his muscular frame. In the almost weightless medium of the crystal pool Brian had infinite control over her body. While he held her close his tantalizing hands kneaded the soft flesh of her buttocks, and then he began to move her against him twisting her gently this way and that so that their water-smooth flesh touched at hip, then breast, then thigh, and then brushed teasingly away again. A riot of sensation rippled through Rowan's pleasure-drugged being as she clung to him. The cool water only emphasized the fiery heat of the blood coursing through her veins.

Brian's fingers were not still either. And when he found her most sensitive secret, her whole body tightened with the mounting excitement of her reaction.

"Brian . . . Brian, I can't stand it," she cried, tugging at his shoulders to communicate her spiraling need.

But he only held her firmly by the waist with one hand and stroked her intimately with the other until she was half-crazed with the sensation. When at last he arched her body and entered her fiercely, Rowan was as liquid as the water surrounding them. She was a molten, seething pit of excitement. As Brian's plunging masculinity stirred her to frenzy, she responded like dynamite to lit gunpowder. They exploded together in a shower of indescribable color compounded of earth, sky, sunlight, and the wonder of Brian's hard, controlled body.

When it was over, she lay resting damply against his heaving chest, feeling the thrum of his heart as he filled his lungs with deep, satisfying breaths.

"So perfect," he murmured lovingly in her ear, his voice a husky caress. "Rowan, we are so perfect together. You must see that now."

In answer she could only touch her lips to his strong neck and close her eyes. He was right. Any further denial was impossible.

The rest of that long, exquisite day went by in a dream

for Rowan. Lost in the clasp of Brian's arms on her waist and shoulders, she hardly noticed the walk back to the cabin. And that night, when they made love again, her love-sated mind could take in only the fact of her contentment and joy in the closeness of Brian's strong embrace.

CHAPTER NINE

It was barely light when Rowan opened her eyes the next morning. Turning her face to one side, she focused on the dark tendrils of hair curling at the base of Brian's cleanly sculpted neck. Delicately she reached out to wind one of the wayward strands around her finger. It clung to her skin, as if trying to hold her fast. And she desperately wanted to be bound to this man.

The slight contact made Brian stir in his sleep. "Rowan," he murmured tenderly and turned to face her in the bed. Though he was still asleep, his body sought hers, curling deftly around her like a protective shell. After their mutual passion had finally been spent last night, he had not turned away, sheltering her instead with his warmth. His sleep had been easy and untroubled, his breathing strong and quiet. But Rowan had lain awake in his arms for hours, not daring to move lest she disturb him. Only when Brian had finally rolled over to his side of the bed in the small hours of the morning had she finally drifted into an uneasy slumber. But now once again she was wide awake.

So much had changed for Rowan in the last twenty-four hours. She no longer cared about Brian's business dealings. Unlike the way she'd felt toward Charles, she knew that she was committed to Brian regardless of what he might have done. But, in any case, she could no longer believe that he was capable of the kind of treachery Bill had hinted at. He would prove himself innocent. She knew it now. For she knew him intimately. And had no doubts about the metal of his character. It was steel, straight and true, but tempered with sensitivity and gentleness.

And she was in love with him as she never had been with any man before—totally and completely. She was in love the way they sang about in popular songs and wrote about in poems. Brian was everything she'd ever dreamed of in a man. In his arms she'd found heights of ecstasy she'd never believed possible. Until now she'd taken all those songs and poems with a grain of salt. But now she knew they spoke the glorious truth. But that wasn't all. It wasn't just his fantastic lovemaking. It was his warmth and humor, the gentleness she'd found along with his strength. And she knew that all the things that had seemed important before were as nothing compared to her relationship with him.

If only she hadn't jeopardized it so stupidly. Once more her heart began to pound in her throat as her mind went back to the morning before, when she'd taken Brian's key to the radio shed. She'd give anything now to replay that scene. If she had the chance to do it all again, she would have stayed beside him and never left his bed. Wincing, she squeezed her eyes closed as though that would shut out the memory of what she had done. But maybe it was still all right, she comforted herself. Nothing had happened yet. And it was a long shot that Bill would get the message in any case.

Once more Brian rolled over, and she was alone on her side of the bed. There was no hope of getting back to sleep now, she knew, twisting the edge of the sheet with nervous fingers. She was too agitated to lose herself in sleep. What she wanted was physical action—to pace the floor and wring her hands while she worked out the problem of whether or not to confess what she'd done to Brian.

But she could hardly pace in the cabin. She would surely wake him up. Maybe a walk along the shore would do as well. She gave her lover a doubtful look. Brian had asked her not to leave his side. But he too had gotten very little sleep that night. Probably she could slip away and return without his ever knowing.

Inching toward the side of the bed, she shifted her weight very gradually. As her feet found the floor Brian stirred again but did not awaken. Tenderly she looked down at him. The rumpled sheet covered his body only to the waist. And his broad, hair-matted chest rose and fell with a peaceful rhythm. Rowan had to stifle an impulse to reach out and stroke the smooth, tan skin of his shoulder. She knew the feel of those powerful shoulders pressing her down into the mattress as he thrust with thrilling male vigor into the enveloping haven of her femininity.

It was all she could do to keep from climbing back into the warm shelter of the bed with him. But she was too uneasy for that. Shivering in the chilly morning air, she pulled on a sweatshirt he'd found for her and stepped into her over-large cutoffs. Ignoring the goosebumps pebbling her legs, she padded quietly to the door, opened it with infinite care, and slipped out into the soft early morning light. A fine mist was rising off the water. And the air had a clean, just-washed feel about it. Washington, with all its scandal and intrigue, might as well have been a million miles away. This island was so pure, untouched by the exigencies of the real world. As she had on that first day, she couldn't help feeling a bit like Eve in the Garden. But a tremor ran through her body as she drew out the analogy. Eve had ruined her Eden with her transgression. Had she, Rowan, done the same by betraying Brian's trust?

Almost physically pushing the disturbing image from her mind, Rowan hunched her shoulders and walked slowly down to the shore with her arms crossed protectively around her chest. Her head was bent in deep thought as she let her toes sink into the soft dirt and then plodded forward to the dark rocks at the water's edge. The feel of the waves lapping against her bare feet sent more shivers up her spine. Again she asked herself what she was going to do. Brian would surely be angry if she told him about the radio message. If she said nothing, maybe he would never find out. But, on the other hand, if she said nothing and he discovered the truth on his own, that would be far worse.

Rowan lowered herself onto a flat rock and sat cross-legged, staring out over the sparkling water as though it might somehow divulge the answer she sought. Slowly the sun climbed, burning away the mist. The dark green of the trees and blue of the sky and water came into bright relief. It was going to be another gorgeous day in paradise.

Suddenly with that thought her mind was made up. If she wanted to remain in Eden—not just this glorious physical place, but by Brian's side wherever he might go—she had to be honest with him. She would wake him now and tell him everything and hope that things would still be all right between them. Jumping to her feet, she turned to head back to the cabin. But at that moment the distant drone of a motor disrupted the lake's early morning tranquility.

Rowan stiffened and turned her tousled head to scan the shimmering surface. At first she could see nothing. But as her eyes strained toward the source of the intruding sound, the tiny black form of a speedboat took shape in the distance. Rowan's brows knitted as she stared at the interloper. She tried to hope it was just passing by, someone out on a fishing trip perhaps. But she had to abandon that hope because she could already tell it was heading straight for Brian's domain.

It had grown from a dark spot to a blue outline that showed the silhouettes of two men leaning forward and gesturing in her direction. One was tall and thin, the other shorter and heavier.

Rowan stood rooted to the spot, unable to move. The faint throb had become a loud roar. And the features of the two men had become distinct. The tall man was Paul

Burton. The short, rounder figure was that of Wally Harding, Bill Emory's ace reporter.

At the beginning of the week Rowan would have been relieved to see his ruddy, blunt-featured face. Although he was a blazing male chauvinist who treated her like the office gofer, she had been able to pick up a lot of pointers from his stories about his exploits. But now his all-too-familiar visage made Rowan's heart rise in her throat and her skin grow clammy. Still her legs would not work. And she didn't know what to do with them anyway. Should she run back to the cabin and warn Brian? Or should she stay and brazen it out? Was there any chance of convincing Paul and Wally that her distress call had been a terrible mistake—that they should turn back and leave without her?

But any hope of reprieve was shattered as Paul cut the motor and the aluminum boat slammed inexpertly against the frail wood dock.

"Just like in the James Bond movies," Wally crowed, his broad cheeks bright red with excitement and exertion. He shot her a triumphant half-moon smile that seemed to split his round face. "Hop in, baby."

The sound of his irritating joviality released Rowan from her spell and she backed away at an angle from the cabin, shaking her head. "Wally, there—there's been a terrible misunderstanding," she stammered.

"No misunderstanding, Rowan," Wally countered, flapping his arms cheerfully as he lumbered heavily out onto the dock while Paul held on to one of the pilings. Even while she framed another protest Rowan was inwardly thinking how little this team resembled the smooth operators from a Bond movie. Brian's comparison to the bumbling Maxwell Smart was more apt, though Wally did have a way of pulling even the wildest misadventures out of the fire, despite his outward cloddishness.

"We got your message loud and clear," he chortled now. "Good work, Row, old girl. How did you manage it?" Without waiting for an answer, Wally galloped the fifty feet that separated them and seized her wrist, obviously intending to propel her toward the boat. "We have to get out of here fast, kid, so shake your pretty little buns," he ordered.

But Rowan pulled back stubbornly. "Wally," she began, "You're not listening to me at all. This is all a terrible mistake."

"You're damn right it is," an all-too-familiar voice snarled behind her. Wally dropped Rowan's wrist as she whirled to see Brian stalking rapidly down the path from the cabin. "Suppose the two of you tell me what the hell's going on, before I throw you off for trespassing."

"What are you going to do, call the Canadian Mounties and have us arrested?" Wally shouted derisively. "That's a laugh. You're the one who's going to be behind bars when that Senate committee gets through with you, Turner. And, by the way, kidnaping is another federal offense to add to your list."

Brian's stark gaze flickered contemptuously away from Wally's squat, belligerent form and focused on Rowan. "What's this fool talking about? How did these two creeps get here?"

As he stared fixedly into Rowan's pale face she tried desperately to collect her scattered wits and give him an answer that wouldn't make him hate her. Neither of them took any notice of Paul. Sizing up the situation, Wally's young companion had thrown a loop of rope over one of the pilings and made the boat fast. Stealthily he began to make his way up the dock. None of the figures locked in verbal conflict on the beach paid any attention to his progress as he made a wide circle up the shoreline that brought him up to the right of Brian and behind him.

"I—I called them," Rowan admitted, flushing miserably. "I was going to tell you . . ."

Her voice died as she watched Brian's dark eyes register

135

incredulity, then bitter contempt. The scathing look he shot her seemed to wither her very soul.

"That's right," Wally chimed in with a well-timed jeer in his voice. "This little lady has made an ass out of you, Turner. How did she get to use your radio—steal the key when you were asleep?" he went on with a loud guffaw. The idea seemed to catch his fancy. "And just how did she get close enough to you to do that?" he leered, coming horribly close to the mark.

Brian went pale beneath his tan. And then a dark red flush spread across his high cheekbones. He balled his fists. A muscle jumping ominously in his cheek, he began to stalk toward Wally.

Wally had learned to recognize a dangerous opponent when he saw one. The shorter man instinctively took a protective step backwards. "No need to get uptight," he said hastily.

Rowan looked wide-eyed back and forth between the two antagonists. Just then a flicker of movement at the corner of her field of vision made her turn her head. It was Paul, one arm clutching a mean-looking driftwood club and raised above his head.

"My God!" Rowan shrieked. "Brian!" But it was already too late. In a blur of motion Paul's lanky body rushed forward. Brian half-turned toward his assailant. But at that moment Paul's weapon came crashing down on his unprotected skull. It was only because Rowan's warning had made him turn slightly that the full force of Paul's blow was deflected slightly.

Rowan heard a wail of horror escape her own mouth. "Brian!" she screamed again, rushing forward to his limp form. He had fallen sideways into a tangle of driftwood, and his right leg was twisted under his body. How badly had Paul hurt him? she thought wildly. Did he need medical attention?

Kneeling down, she felt the goose egg forming on the

back of his head. And one of her hands went to his neck, where, to her relief, she felt a strong, steady pulse.

Both Wally and Paul had followed her over and were hovering in the background.

"He's okay," Paul said, to reassure himself as much as Rowan. "He'll be coming to in a few minutes."

"And we'd better be out of here before he does," Wally added.

Rowan looked up at Wally with pleading eyes. "But you can't just leave him like this," she protested. "His leg might be broken."

Wally squatted next to her and straightened out the twisted leg. Still unconscious, Brian groaned, and Rowan's heart turned over.

"It's not broken, just sprained. These prep school types are made of rubber. He shouldn't have any trouble getting back to the cabin when he comes to. But if it'll make you feel any better, there's a radio on the boat. And I'll alert the authorities as soon as we're out of the area."

In the face of Wally's cavalier dismissal Rowan's pleading turned to anger.

"You bastard!" she spat out. "You're no doctor. You don't know how badly he's hurt. I refuse to let you leave him."

It was the wrong approach to take with her chauvinistic colleague. He turned to Paul and, with his blunt hands on his square, wide-set hips, began to talk about her as if she weren't there.

"Just like a broad. She's hysterical. I don't know what Turner did to her. But for her own good we'll have to get her out of here right now."

"He didn't do anything to me—" Rowan began to sputter.

Ignoring her furious protests, as though she were nothing but an hysterical child, the two men turned to each other. "You grab her legs and I'll get her shoulders," Wally directed maddeningly.

137

He might as well be talking about a sack of potatoes. Is this really happening? But when Wally's beefy hands unceremoniously dug in behind her shoulders and clamped under her armpits, she knew it was no illusion.

"Now this is for your own good, Row. So just relax and stop struggling," he muttered. The effect of his patronizing tone was to make Rowan's temper explode through her ears.

"Get your clammy hands off me, you clown!" she shrieked, struggling to elude Paul's reluctant attempts to capture her ankles. Kicking for all she was worth, she landed several well-placed blows on his arms and chest.

"Grab the wildcat's legs, for God's sake!" Wally shouted.

"Easy for you to say!" Paul puffed, finally managing to seize a flailing ankle. "She's not threatening your masculinity!"

Even when Paul finally had both of her ankles, Rowan didn't make it any easier for them. Wildly she flexed her legs and shoulder muscles. And her mouth wasn't still either as she cursed the pair all the way down the dock.

"Did you realize that she knew all these four-letter words?" Wally asked Paul in a shocked voice as they swung her over the side and into the boat. "I tell you, she's full of surprises. I never dreamed that angelic mouth could utter such vile expletives. You better sit on her, Paul, while I start the motor."

Paul proceeded to do just that, turning a fuming Rowan over on her stomach and squatting on top of her so that his bony haunches pinned her down.

"Better hurry," Paul panted as Wally struggled with the motor cord. "I can't keep this up for long. She's tossing around so much she's making me seasick."

"I'll make you worse than seasick," she threatened in a strangled voice as she fought, despite Paul's weight, to lever herself up. "You deserve to be—" But the violent conclusion of her sentence was cut off as the outboard motor sputtered and then sprang to life.

Wally gave the dock a shove that nosed the bow of the small craft away and then opened the throttle. As the vessel leaped forward and raced away from shore he leaned over and shouted into Rowan's ear, "Your boyfriend was coming to just as we left, so he's not dead. Now sit up and start behaving like a lady." Rowan ground her teeth and glared in his direction.

"I'll behave like a lady when you start behaving like a human being, you creep! Now turn this boat around!"

Wally sighed elaborately and shook his head at Paul, as if to underline the lunatic incorrigibility of the whole female sex. Leaning forward once more, he made another attempt to reason. "I'm not going anywhere but back to D.C., Row. And if you keep jumping around under poor old Paul this way, you'll overturn us and we'll drown. And then," he added with morbid triumph, "I won't be able to call a doctor for lover boy."

Even in Rowan's agitated state, Wally's little speech made sense. It was clear there was nothing she could do to change his mind. All she could hope was that someone would come to Brian's aid and that he really wasn't seriously injured. What's more, she admitted to herself, she really couldn't go on this way much longer. She was already exhausted. Her face was bright red with exertion and the blood that had rushed to her head was clanging in her ears like a firebell.

"All right," she gritted. "Let me up and I'll cooperate."

Wally raised an unruly eyebrow. "No tricks?"

Rowan gave him a baleful look and then sighed. "No tricks. But you'd better get on that radio right now!"

Gingerly Paul shifted his weight and allowed his prisoner to sit up uncomfortably. She was stiff and sore all over from her exertions.

"That's better," Wally said with false heartiness. "I'll break out the CB as soon as we're out of Canadian waters." His words reassured her somewhat, but that brief respite was destroyed by his next remark. "What a great story this is going to make!" he crowed ecstatically. "I can just see the front page headlines now!"

Slowly, agonizingly, Brian's hand went to the back of his head. The shaft of pain that shot through his skull as he touched the gigantic lump that was throbbing there made him groan aloud. Somewhere through the fog of pain he was conscious of angry voices. But he was incapable of focusing on anything but the battering ram that seemed to be at work inside his head. The voices receded farther into the background, and he tried to open his eyes. When he succeeded, the sunlight slanting through the trees caused another piercing twinge and he snapped them shut.

One of the rapidly fading voices belonged to Rowan, he suddenly realized. She was saying something in a high-pitched shriek that made his eyes snap open again. Regardless of the pain, he had to find out what was going on. Struggling to roll over, he reached out blindly and seized one of the driftwood branches that formed his uncomfortable resting place. But the loose stick came free in his hand and he fell backward with a curse. The impact of his already-abused head making contact with the hard ground was excruciating. And he was becoming aware of another throbbing pain—in his ankle. It must be injured as well, he told himself, trying desperately to sit up and finally succeeding. But his reward for the enormous effort was small. As he lifted his arm to screen out the blinding sun an outboard motor roared. Gradually the aluminum fishing boat that had brought the two interlopers swam into focus. But before he could see the craft clearly, it was already receding into the distance.

He looked bleakly around at the deserted shoreline. It was empty. Then he realized just how empty as his gaze went once more to the glint of silver disappearing into the horizon. Rowan was on that boat. And then he remembered the fat one's insulting insinuations about the key to the radio shack. The SOB must have been right. Somehow Rowan had stolen the key and used the radio to send for them. Brian's hand went to his forehead, and he whistled through his teeth disdainfully. There was only one way she would have been able to get the key out of his pants pocket undetected. And that was by taking it while he slept naked at her side.

The realization hurt even more than the blinding throbbing in his head, and for the third time he groaned aloud. He had trusted her, shared his most intimate feelings with her, and she had callously betrayed him. His firm lips drew back in a grimace. He'd thought Rowan was something special. Well, she was something special all right. There was a name for women like that. But he'd considered himself too experienced to be taken in by one. Well, he'd never make that mistake again. Not with Rowan Strickland—that was for damn sure!

Forcing his arms to work for him, he heaved himself up to his knees and then, using a rough piece of driftwood as a cane, he struggled to his feet. It was almost impossible to put any weight on the injured foot. Brian took a deep breath. It was going to be a long trip back to the cabin—and an even harder one up the hill to the radio shed. His dark eyes glanced once more out at the now empty lake. An image of Rowan as she had looked swimming almost naked off the dock flashed treacherously into his mind. Ruthlessly he banished it and then turned toward the cabin.

CHAPTER TEN

Numbly Rowan huddled in the bottom of the boat. *This isn't happening. It can't be true,* she told herself over and over. But it was true. Her ribs hurt where Wally had manhandled her. And she rubbed them gingerly with the flat of her palms.

"I'm sorry, baby," Wally apologized, taking note of her exploring hands. "I didn't mean to rough you up. But you wouldn't listen to reason back there on the beach. That Turner must be one fantastic lover to have turned you into a bowl of Jell-O so fast." The speech which had begun as a weak apology ended as a typical piece of Wally's callousness.

Rowan looked up sharply, aware that her cheeks were turning pink and that both men were observing the effect with interest. Her reaction, she knew, was confirmation of Wally's ungentlemanly speculations. Yes, Brian had been a fantastic lover, and much more. But she certainly wasn't going to discuss their relationship with these two.

Meeting Wally's eyes, she glared at him with the full force of her bridled fury. "Listen," she began, emphasizing her words so that her message would come through loud and clear. "If you want even a modicum of cooperation from me, shut your foul mouth. What happened between Brian Turner and me is none of your business."

Looks of surprise and then caution chased themselves across Wally's beefy face. He opened his mouth to speak and then, changing his mind, snapped it shut again.

"Better let up, Wally," Paul cautioned. "She's about to blow her top again. And we don't want that."

Rowan turned and glared at him. He shrugged and busied himself with coiling the rope that lay in the bottom of the boat. Wally had pulled out a navigational chart and began to study it with a great show of interest. And Rowan was suddenly left alone with her thoughts.

Slumping down on one of the metal thwarts, she rested her elbows on her knees and propped her chin in her hands. An image of Brian lying unconscious in the driftwood flashed painfully into her consciousness. Instinctively she screwed her eyes shut to try and banish the terrible picture. But it lingered before her closed eyes nevertheless like a brightly colored transparency projected on the wall of a lecture hall. The picture was frightening in its clarity, and suddenly Rowan realized that Wally still hadn't made his emergency call. Right now she wanted nothing to do with the obnoxious reporter, but it looked as though the only way the call would get made would be through her intercession. Straightening she cleared her throat.

Both men looked apprehensively in her direction. But the defeated sag of her shoulders told them that for the moment they had nothing more to fear.

"Will you make that SOS call for Brian now?" she asked, fighting to keep her voice from cracking.

"Sure," Wally agreed with a surprising show of cooperation. "Paul, you take the helm while I break out the CB. Lucky this is the only thing we had to use it for," he added under his breath as the two men awkwardly changed places.

Rowan listened carefully while Wally made the call. When it was completed, she sank back into herself. They were in a much more thickly populated stretch of the river now, with many islands dotting the blue water. But Rowan took no notice of the picturebook scenery. Nothing really seemed to matter. Not her surroundings. Nor the ache of her ribs. Nor the expressions of triumph on the faces of her colleagues.

She was only conscious of the heavy sense of misery that seem to weigh her down like an anchor hopelessly tangled in seaweed.

The ride seemed endless. And several times she heard Wally curse as he consulted his charts. "These damn channels here are like a maze," he complained to Paul as once more he was forced to put the boat in reverse and back out of an inlet that he had mistakenly thought led to open water.

It was long after she had refused Paul's offer of crushed peanut butter sandwiches and warm beer that she heard the motor cut to half-throttle again.

"Alexandria Bay," Paul announced as Rowan stared blankly at the rows of low buildings hugging the shoreline. "Bolt Castle is right across the channel," he intoned in the authoritative voice of a tour guide.

But Rowan didn't even bother to look up at the picturesque red stone ruin George Bolt had begun building for his beloved wife. Inconsolable after her death, he had abandoned the massive project. But Rowan was much too absorbed in her own misery to take much notice. And that set the tone for the rest of the day.

The cunning little town of Alexandria Bay, designed to separate tourists from as much of their money as possible, never captured her interest. And though sightseers waiting on the dock for the next tour boat to the castle stared at her disheveled appearance, she was oblivious.

"We're attracting too much attention," Wally whispered to Paul after they'd returned the boat and left the dock behind. "Barefoot and in those ragged cutoffs, she looks like a groupie left over from Woodstock."

Paul pointed out a small apparel shop, and together they guided Rowan inside, where they picked out a pair of jeans, a pink T-shirt, and a pair of sandals. When she'd obediently donned the outfit they'd selected, Paul even whipped out a comb and tried to smarten up her curls. But the touch of his hand on her shoulder made her cringe, and he quickly shoved it back in his shirt pocket.

"The airport around here isn't much. But it isn't far either," Wally muttered encouragingly as they shepherded her back out onto the street. "We'll grab a cab and head out there right away. No sense in hanging around here."

"You'll feel better when we get back to D.C.," Wally assured as if he'd read her mind. "You'll see. Everything will be different back home."

But he was wrong. Everything felt wrong, starting with the impact of the capital city's famous heat and humidity. When she stepped out of the plane at National Airport, the muggy air settled around her like a wet wool blanket in a steamroom.

"Listen, Rowan," Wally offered as they maneuvered through the crowd in the terminal building. "Bill told me to bring you straight to his office. But you look like a zombie, so we'll stop at your apartment. You can catch a shower and a quick nap. Maybe that will perk you up."

At that moment Rowan was too exhausted to express her gratitude. But after Wally had talked the superintendent into opening her front door, and she was once more in the familiar eclectic warmth of her small apartment, she had to blink to keep the tears from spilling from her eyes.

"Go take a shower," Wally ordered gruffly, "and then get some shut-eye. If it will make you feel any better, I'll call Bill. He's got someone monitoring your boyfriend's radio frequency now. Maybe we can find out what's been happening up there."

Rowan sat down on a chair. "Make the call right now," she urged. Wally complied. She heard him speaking to Bill in low tones. After putting down the receiver, he turned back to her.

"Brian Turner has made a call to one of his cronies, who's on his way to pick him up now. So you can relax and stop worrying about him being dead."

Rowan felt as though a great weight had lifted from her chest. Finally she felt free to take care of her own needs. Head bent, she nodded almost imperceptibly and then disappeared into the bathroom, locking the door behind her. In her present state of numb exhaustion the steamy water of the shower was a soporific. After pulling on the blue chenille robe that hung on the hook near the tub, she almost staggered back into her room. Rowan crawled gratefully between the crisp sheets on her four-poster bed. She had only to shut her eyes to plummet into merciful unconsciousness.

But only two hours later she was hauled back from the deep well of oblivion into which she had sunk by the sound of raucous male voices.

For a moment she lay there disoriented, blinking groggily. Even in the dim evening light the familiar surroundings told her she was home in her apartment. But what were those men doing in her kitchen? she asked herself with growing alarm.

However, the voices quickly began to separate themselves into familiar patterns. Over the clink of cutlery and glasses she recognized the gruff tones of Bill Emory and Wally Harding, along with Paul Burton's excited tenor.

She had assumed Wally and Paul would leave after dropping her off. But they had apparently stayed around and made themselves right at home—and invited their boss to join them. What was going on, anyway? she asked herself, throwing back the covers and stepping onto the oriental rug beside her bed. Tiptoeing across the room, she made sure the door was locked and then snapped on the light. It took only a minute to throw on jeans and a sleeveless knit top. Looking at herself in the dresser mirror, she grimaced. Almost a week in the wilds had given her skin a healthy tan. But it hadn't done anything for her Raggedy Ann mop of curls. However, there wasn't much she could do about that now, she realized after fighting with her hairbrush for a few minutes. Anyway, what did that matter? she asked herself. She really wasn't interested in impressing the three gentlemen who were out there making free with her kitchen.

Just then she heard the sound of crockery shattering on the tile floor accompanied by a richly expressive curse.

Dropping the hairbrush, Rowan wheeled around and threw open the bedroom door. Marching through the living room, she almost stumbled over Wally, who was down on his hands and knees in the dinette. He was sweeping up the shattered remains of her favorite pitcher.

Paul and Bill, who were seated comfortably at her round oak table spooning up kung pao chicken from white cardboard cartons, looked up guiltily.

"Sorry, Row," Bill apologized. "Wally got a little overenthusiastic while he was describing the showdown with Turner."

At the mention of the morning's fiasco Rowan's eyes began to sparkle with renewed anger.

Misinterpreting her reaction, Bill jumped hastily from his seat. "Let me get a wet paper towel and help him," he offered. "You can buy another one of these and charge it to me."

"It's not the kind of thing you can get in a department store," Rowan clipped out. "It's a nineteenth-century Staffordshire milk jug I picked up at an auction."

Paul had the grace to look down at his moo goo gai pan sheepishly, but Wally was unrepentant. "What do you buy that old stuff for?"

"And what business is that of yours?" Rowan shot back. "And while we're on the subject, why are you helping yourselves to my kitchen and my dishes anyway?"

The three men exchanged glances. And then Bill thrust an unopened carton in her direction. "Buddhist's delight," he offered. "One of your favorites."

"Maybe it'll mellow you out," Wally added under his breath.

Rowan inspected the carton with jaundiced eyes. But it

was her favorite, and she was hungry. "All right," she muttered, pulling out a bentwood chair and sitting down. As Paul poured her a cup of Chinese tea she opened the white container and spooned the fragrant vegetable combination onto a plate. The delicious aroma made her realize just how starved she was, and soon she'd finished half the serving. She was grateful for the dinner, but she wasn't going to let her gratitude mollify her. "What are you guys doing here?" she demanded, looking up from her plate.

Paul refilled her cup. "Waiting for you to wake up so we can talk."

"About what?" Rowan forked up another baby corncob and put it in her mouth.

Wally snorted impatiently. "About Brian Turner, of course. You do recall that he kidnaped you and kept you captive for almost a week?"

Rowan chewed thoughtfully. But though she was keeping her face blank, her mind was working overtime. "What about it?" she said at last.

Bill threw up his hands. "Look, Rowan, it's a terrific story. We want the details so we can go to press with it before anyone else does. You've been out of touch so you don't know what's been going on. Ever since Turner disappeared, the newspapers have been going crazy. This has got to be the story of the decade, and you're sitting right on top of it. Now give!"

Rowan put her fork down and gave her boss an anguished look. "Bill, I have to try and make you understand. Things have changed for me. I'm absolutely convinced that Brian Turner is innocent. And if we break a story like this, we'll only end up looking like fools when he proves he's not guilty."

Wally tilted his chair back and rolled his eyes ceilingward. "See, didn't I tell you?" he burst out. "She's been brainwashed. Turner's got her thinking he's Peter Pan, Santa Claus, and the Easter Bunny all rolled into one."

"Lay off," Paul muttered. "She's had a rough time."
But Bill cut him short.

"Rowan, you are a newspaperwoman, a professional employed by me to do a job. I'm sorry to have to put it this way, but you *are* going to do that job—whether you like it or not. Now quit stalling and give us that information." He opened his briefcase and withdrew a small tape recorder. Arranging it on the table with elaborate precision, he inserted a tape and clicked the machine on. Then he turned back and gave her a long, frosty stare.

It took all of Rowan's control to still her trembling chin. She was fond of Bill and she respected him. Under normal circumstances they were always on the same side. But these circumstances were definitely not normal.

Even if it meant losing her job, she must not betray Brian again. Stealing the key had been a terrible mistake, and she wasn't going to compound it with another. Slowly she raised her eyes until they met his, then she shook her head. "I'm sorry, Bill. I'm not going to do it. You're just going to have to trust my judgment this time."

"Damnit, Rowan!" Bill slammed the flat of his hand onto the table, making the recorder jump from the impact. And Rowan herself was so startled that she shrank back defensively in her chair, almost toppling it over. Bill's ruddy complexion had turned several shades darker, and she could almost picture his blood pressure shooting upward.

"Please . . ." she began.

But her plea was cut short by an oath from Wally. He had gotten up from the table and was pacing the length of the small dinette with impatient strides. "Women," he muttered derisively, slapping his balled fist into the flat of his hand. "If I live to be a hundred, I'll never understand them." He shot Rowan an injured look. "She sent us a distress call, and we moved heaven and earth to get up there and save her. So what thanks do we get?" He opened his arms in a gesture of emptiness and frustration.

Rowan bit her lip and looked down. From his point of view none of this made any sense. She did owe them some sort of explanation. But explaining her jumbled feelings was almost impossible. "Wally, you just don't understand. Brian Turner isn't the sort of person you think. He's honorable; I just know it. There's got to be some reasonable explanation for this computer chip business. I know there's something funny going on in his company," she rushed on, "but I heard enough of his discussions with his colleagues to know that he's got private detectives at work trying to find out what it is. Now why would he do that if he were guilty?" she asked, trying to appeal to his sense of logic.

Wally shook his head impatiently. "How should I know? Maybe he was just putting on a little performance for an all-too-appreciative audience of one—you."

Wally looked at his boss and raised his eyebrows meaningfully. Bill slowly shook his head. "You're right about the brainwashing," he conceded. "I believe this is going to take some deprogramming on our part. Let's start with yesterday's *Washington Post* editorial on Mr. Wonderful. Maybe when Rowan has had a chance to look through some of these news stories, she'll revise her opinion."

Fumbling in his briefcase again, Bill pulled out a thick folder of newspaper clippings and set them on the table to one side of her plate. Glancing down, she saw that the food was now cold and congealed. But it didn't matter. She'd lost her appetite. She couldn't believe what was happening. These men had apparently decided to be Brian Turner's judge and jury. They had already found him guilty. And no amount of logical persuasion was going to change their minds.

Their campaign to bring Rowan around to their way of thinking started off mildly enough with newspaper clippings. But it soon escalated. For the next two days she became a virtual hostage in her apartment while the three men took turns cajoling, reasoning, and finally haranguing. There was no chance of escape. One of them was always awake—guarding against just such an eventuality.

For the first time she got a taste of what it was like to be on the wrong side of one of Bill's crusades. But through it all she stubbornly held out. Every move of his was countered by a gesture of defiance on her part.

It was a grim time for Rowan. Only the loyalty she felt to Brian kept her from caving in. Often she was on the verge of tears. But she was determined not to show Bill or Wally her feminine "weakness." And so she channeled her distress into defiance. Finally, when Bill, in exasperation, threatened to fire her, she angrily dashed off a written resignation and flung it in his face.

Ironically the battle of wills ended as it had begun—with a newspaper article—this time the lead story in the *Washington Post.*

"My God, look at this!" Paul exclaimed as he brought in the paper on the third morning of their seige. "Rowan was right all along. Turner has been vindicated."

"Lemme see that," Bill growled, snatching the paper out of the younger man's hands. Rowan watched his mouth drop open as he scanned the front page story. "Well, I'll be dammed," he muttered, scratching the back of his head and then tossing the paper in her direction.

Picking it up off the table, Rowan read the story, quoting phrases as she progressed. "Totally cleared of all charges . . . Head of marketing responsible for misdirecting computer chips to unfriendly nations in payoff scheme . . . full confession after discovery by Turner's team of private investigators . . . Turner takes partial responsibility, admitting he should have been on top of the situation earlier, but officials exonerate him of any culpability in the matter."

Triumphantly she looked up at the three men who now confronted her sheepishly.

"I don't know what to say," Bill began. "You were absolutely right, Row. If we'd published that story about you and Turner, we'd have egg on our faces this morning."

The sudden silence in the room was so thick that Rowan could have cut it with the butter knife Wally had set down when she began to read the newspaper article aloud.

One of the only things that had kept her going through her colleagues' interrogation was her loyalty to Brian and the certain knowledge that she would finally prevail. But Bill's apology did not have the effect she had been anticipating. Instead of feeling triumphant, she suddenly felt tired and hollow.

The long ordeal had drained her, she realized, allowing her shoulders to slump for the first time in days as she closed her eyes and sank into a chair, leaning her head back against its comforting softness.

"Rowan," Paul began. "I can't tell you how sorry I am about all of this . . ." But his voice trailed off as he saw the weary blankness of her expression.

Slowly Rowan shook her head. It was too much effort to lift her lids. And, besides, the way she felt now, she never wanted to set eyes on this trio again. "If the three of you really want to do something for me, just leave me alone," she whispered, unable to muster up the energy for anything louder.

They looked at each other and then around the apartment. Uneasily Paul shifted his weight from one foot to the other. Rowan was an orderly person, and three days ago her abode had been immaculate. But now it looked as though a Marine detachment had used it for a bivouac. Scattered about were ashtrays overflowing with Wally's cigarettes and Bill's pungent cigar butts. Cans of beer and half-full glasses littered the tables and decorated the rugs. One tumbler, which had been overturned in the corner, was surrounded by a moon-size yellow stain that stood out boldly against the off-white of her carpeting. Blankets draped over couches and chairs and unwashed dishes stacked on the antique side tables and overflowing the sink added to the disarray. Topping it all off were the file folders and piles of newspaper making a haphazard checkerboard on the floor.

Bill cleared his throat. "Don't you want us to clean up a bit before we leave? I'm afraid we've made sort of a mess."

That was the understatement of the year, Rowan thought as she finally forced her eyes open and gazed dryly around at the disaster that had once been her haven.

"I think you guys have done more than enough," she muttered. "So why don't you just please leave."

Hastily Wally grabbed his jacket. And his companions followed his example.

"Take the day off, Rowan," Bill offered magnanimously as he opened the front door.

That was the last straw. Pushing herself to her feet, Rowan grabbed the first thing her fingers encountered on the table next to her chair. It was a manila folder full of clippings. As she raised it above her head Bill leaped out of the way with more agility than she would have thought possible for a man of his bulk. He slammed the door shut just as the folder slapped against it. And Rowan watched with a feeling of despair as the clippings showered down the painted wood surface and onto the floor.

Rowan stared at this newly created mess for a moment and then sank back into the chair, lowering her head and raising her trembling hands to her face. All the tears she had been holding back since she'd been dragged away from Brian suddenly came spilling out. They drenched her cheeks and flowed between her fingers, but they didn't make her feel any better—only more exhausted. She cried until there were no more tears left, only dry, racking sobs. Shakily she stumbled to her feet. She wanted to crawl into bed, pull the covers over her head, and stay there for a month.

CHAPTER ELEVEN

Twenty-four hours later the shrilling of the phone broke the heavy stillness in Rowan's blue and white bedroom. Groggily her limp hand reached out to fumble for the receiver and press it to her ear.

"Um . . ." she mumbled.

"Rowan?" Bill's voice was asking. "Are you still asleep?"

"Uh-huh, I guess so."

There was a pause, which Rowan used to drag herself into a half-sitting position.

"I expected to hear from you before now. Are you all right?"

Was she? she wondered, groggily considering the question. At this point she didn't know. "How long have I been asleep?" she asked.

"If you went to bed right after we left, the answer is twenty-four hours."

That made her sit up straight. "Twenty-four hours? You mean it's Wednesday already?"

Bill chuckled. "Okay, Sleeping Beauty, I have a bulletin for you. I've hired a maid service to clean your apartment. They ought to be arriving in an hour. So get dressed. But close your eyes on the way to the front door. I'll be there to take you out to brunch while they clean up." She could tell from the tone of his voice that he was pleased with himself. Though she was still upset and wondered if she would ever really forgive him, Rowan was not the kind of

154

person who held onto her anger in a self-destructive fashion. And right now she had more to gain by going along with Bill than by making war on him, no matter what he had done to her.

"Okay," she finally agreed. "I ought to meet you at the door with a raised club, but I'm feeling too weak for that. So I'll settle for depleting your bank account at a restaurant instead." Her facetious threat apparently struck just the right note with Bill. His rich laughter echoed in Rowan's ear. "In that case we'll go to the Jockey Club. That will give you lots of room to maneuver."

The long sleep had refreshed Rowan enough that her mind began to function once again. While she showered and dressed to meet Bill she told herself that there were some questions she had to ask. This whole misbegotten affair had put serious doubts in her mind about her job and her direction in life. Ultimately, she knew, things could be worked out with Bill. Brian was the big question. What would his attitude be toward her now? Would he still want her? She knew from the newspapers he'd been back in Washington for two days. But he hadn't called. The sudden realization made her heart lurch. She couldn't live with uncertainty where he was concerned. She had to know now what his feelings were. Decisively she went to the phone book next to her bed and looked up Turner Enterprises. But when she dialed the number of the Washington office, all she got was an answering service. Not wanting to leave a message, she hung up. The phone in his apartment must be unlisted. Rowan bit her lip. Maybe there was a favor Bill could do her. And he certainly owed her one now, she assured herself.

Her apologetic boss arrived flanked by two burly men in coveralls wielding vacuum cleaners, mops, and industrial-strength floor polish.

"Mighty Maids, Limited," Bill explained, gesturing at the formidable twosome. "And I think they've got their work cut out for them, so let's leave them to it."

As he escorted her to the elevator Bill gave her a comprehensive once-over. "You look good in that dress. Blue suits you."

Rowan shrugged. Bill might want to pretend this was business as usual, but she was far from back to normal yet. "I just threw on the first decent thing I found in my closet," she informed him. "But thanks anyway."

On the way to the Jockey Club in a taxi Bill kept up a steady stream of shoptalk. Rowan didn't even pretend to hold up her end of the conversation, but he didn't seem to notice.

However, once they were settled at a quiet table in a corner of the elegant restaurant, her boss cleared his throat and gave his companion a straight look.

"This may sound hard to believe, but you're not the only one who's had a rough time over the last three days."

Rowan shot him a skeptical look, but Bill plowed on regardless.

"Giving you the third degree tore me up inside. You know how I feel about the people on my staff, Rowan. But I was so convinced I was right and you were wrong that I was willing to do almost anything to make you crack."

"Lucky for me thumbscrews aren't standard equipment in the civilized world these days," Rowan remarked.

Bill looked suitably chastened. "I deserved that and anything else you care to dish out. But I want to make you understand something. The last few days have given me a lot to think about. What I did to you was unforgivable. I could see it because you're someone close to me. But it made me start wondering seriously about the tactics I've been using for years now—like bugging Brian Turner's boat, for example. I know a certain amount of questionable maneuvering in this business is unavoidable. But from now on I'm going to give more serious thought to the way I get a story."

Rowan's eyes widened. She had never expected anything like this from the tough and unyielding man who was her boss.

But his next words were even more surprising. "Rowan, I know what's been going through your head. You want to quit. And I don't blame you." It was true, she acknowledged inwardly. She had been thinking seriously of resigning.

At that moment she was spared from answering by the waiter's well-timed appearance. He was carrying Bill's order of veal Oscar and the spinach-mushroom salad she'd requested.

As the dishes were arranged on the table she considered what her answer should be.

But he didn't give her a chance. Once the waiter had faded unobtrusively into the background again, he forestalled her reply. "Don't quit now, Rowan," he appealed. "You've had a bad experience and you're upset. Give things a chance to settle back to normal before you make a decision like that."

Normal, Rowan thought, poking disinterestedly at her salad. How could things ever get back to normal? She had fallen in love with a man whose good opinion she had surely forfeited. Suddenly her chest felt tight. How was she was going to get through this meal? Pushing the salad away, she leaned back in her chair.

"All right, I'll think about it," she told Bill. "I don't know how I'd pay next month's rent anyway if I quit now. But there is something you can do that I would appreciate very much."

Her boss raised a questioning eyebrow.

Before she lost her nerve, she plunged on. "You can get me Brian Turner's unlisted D.C. phone number. I called his office this morning, but it's just an answering service. And . . ." she paused, flushing under Bill's penetrating gaze. "I, uh, I have to talk to him personally."

Bill reached across the table and covered one of her

157

slender hands a large paw. "You weren't protecting him just as a matter of principle, were you?" he asked quietly.

Unable to trust her voice, Rowan bit her lip and shook her head.

Sobering, Bill sat up and put the tips of his fingers together. "That won't be easy," he said. "Everybody in town wants a personal interview with Brian Turner. And he's probably changed his number since he got back. But I've got a contact down at the phone company. And I'll do my best."

And he did. That afternoon, back in her now sparkling-clean apartment, Rowan was trying to fit together the pieces of her broken milk pitcher when the phone rang. It was Bill's secretary with the number she had requested. "He said it cost him a bottle of Scotch and to guard it with your life," the young woman explained. Rowan thanked her and wrote down the seven digits.

But once she held the piece of flowered note paper, her hands began to tremble. This was going to take more courage than she'd realized. "Come on," she told herself aloud, "stop stalling."

But she couldn't still the tremor in her hands when she picked up the receiver again and started to press the buttons. Her breathing was labored in her own ears as she listened to the slow rings on the other end of the line. Her heart had begun to pound, and she felt short of breath. At the fourth ring she began to hope that he wouldn't answer after all. Suddenly she felt totally unprepared to speak. But as she was about to lower the receiver back into its cradle, she heard a peremptory click, followed by Brian's impatient baritone voice.

"Turner here."

At the sound of his dearly familiar voice her heart seemed to turn over. "Brian?" she got out, a little breathlessly.

There was a long silence. She stared down at the receiver. "Brian?" she repeated, even more uncertainly. "Are you okay?"

"How did you get this number?" he rasped, ignoring her question. "The telephone company only gave it to me yesterday." And then inspiration seemed to strike. He barked a harsh laugh. "Oh, but I'd forgotten your truly remarkable talent for prying."

The coldness of his tone sent a shudder up Rowan's spine. She'd guessed he would be angry. But the reality of it now hit her with full force. "Brian," she began hastily, willing her unsteady voice not to crack, "I want to explain about what happened on the island."

"Don't feel you have to explain, Ms. Strickland," he lashed out, his voice scourging her like a whip. "I know exactly what happened on the island. I thought I understood amoral women, but you were certainly an education. I'd say you were really willing to go the distance, weren't you? Well, you won't get another chance. Don't bother to call this number again."

The receiver crashed on the other end of the line and the finality of the sound seemed to reverberate in Rowan's tiny living room. She stared at the instrument in her hand with horror, all the blood slowly draining from her cheeks. The pain he had inflicted with mere words was so sharp that it was like a knife wound. Protectively she wrapped her arms around her rib cage and began to rock back and forth, moaning softly. It seemed as though she ought to feel blood on her clenched fingers. But instead all she felt was a gnawing emptiness that seemed to spread through her whole body.

She hadn't dared let herself anticipate his total rejection, she realized. Somehow she had thought she could make things right between them. But now that his feelings were all too clear, she wondered how she'd been able to imagine he might forgive her. She had been deluding herself. Everything about their parting scene should have prepared her for his scorn. He had learned in the worst possible way that she'd taken the key. She could thank Wally for that. But then she shook her head. Who was she kidding? In the last analysis, it was really her fault. If she had just trusted Brian—if she had just trusted her feelings about him—none of this would have happened. She'd be with him now instead of sitting here alone in an agony of loneliness and longing. Her eyes burned and tears began to trail down her cheeks. My God, he wasn't even going to give her a chance to explain. What was she going to do?

Sometime that night, after she had shed all the tears there were, a bit of her old spark reignited itself. She loved Brian too much to simply accept this harsh dismissal. And there must be some way she could get him back, she told herself. She had to hold on to that idea if she wanted to keep her sanity. But no plan came to mind immediately. And until it did, she needed something to keep herself from wallowing in misery. Tomorrow she'd go back to the office. The work which had accumulated in her absence would occupy her time.

But as she sat at her desk the next morning Brian Turner's name was one of the first things that cropped up.

"Your computer wonder boy is holding a press conference this afternoon to sew up the missing chip caper. Want to cover it?" Bill asked, giving her a searching look.

To keep from meeting his eyes, Rowan looked down at the pile of press releases and reports that had accumulated on her desk. Under any other circumstances she would have leaped at an opportunity to escape from all the boring busywork that would be her lot for the next two or three weeks. But these circumstances were far from normal. Did she really have the courage to face Brian so soon after his scathing rejection? And yet, she reassured herself, a press conference was a public gathering. He could hardly make a scene there. Her emotions and her mind were engaged in a tug of war. She wanted desperately to see Brian. But she felt so unprepared—and afraid.

160

"Is there anyone else you can send?" she asked Bill, trying to sound as businesslike as possible.

He shook his head. "There's only Wally and Paul, but somehow I don't think they'd get through the door."

Despite her emotional turmoil Rowan could see the black humor beyond Bill's mild explanation. "You're right—Wally and Paul are definitely not Brian Turner's favorite people."

Bill picked up a sheaf of press releases from her desk and weighed them with his hand before letting them drop back in a disorderly pile. "Most of this stuff is garbage, Rowan. You know that. Why don't you go? It can't do any harm at this stage."

He was right about that, Rowan reflected. She couldn't be on any worse terms with Brian than she was now. "Okay," she agreed, "I'll do it."

But as it turned out, she was wrong about the depths to which her relationship with her former lover could sink.

That afternoon Rowan chose a seat halfway toward the back on the left in one of the Wardman Park's meeting rooms. Almost fifty reporters had already crowded the richly panelled room, and Rowan was easily able to lose herself in the chattering throng.

"You've got to give the guy credit for having guts," the gray-haired newsman occupying the seat in front of her exclaimed to his companion. "Anybody else would want to sweep this whole thing under the rug. But he's being really up front."

"Yeah," his friend agreed. "His company's stock has already fallen twenty points on the New York Exchange. I wonder how today's little maneuver will affect it."

Rowan hunched her shoulders and looked down at her notebook. She had thought Brian's problems were at an end now that he was vindicated. But obviously that wasn't the case. He was still under a lot of pressure—much of it of his own making. Anyone else *would* have avoided the direct confrontation with the press that Brian had let himself in for today.

However, when the tall, dark-haired executive swept into the room, he bore no signs of stress. His tanned, clean-cut features were impassive, and beneath the expensive, formally tailored dark business suit he wore, his broad shoulders were square. But as he strode quickly up the narrow aisle between the rows of murmuring reporters Rowan did notice with a pang that he had a slight limp. That must be Paul's work, she told herself regretfully.

During the first few minutes of the press conference Rowan was so overwhelmed by Brian's commanding physical presence that she couldn't take in the words of his prepared statement. She loved this man. Seeing him again only confirmed it.

But finally she dragged her errant thoughts back to her task. She was, after all, here on assignment. Taking out her ballpoint, she held it poised above the blank notebook page in her lap. And when Brian began to talk about the details of the computer chip caper, she dutifully noted down the essentials. A barrage of questions followed his opening remarks. Brian fielded these smoothly, even handing out statistics on exactly how many chips had been stolen and where each had ended up. He went on to explain how game chips could be used in any computers and why it would be profitable to divert them to hostile nations. She couldn't help being impressed at the smoothly professional way he handled himself. This was a new facet of his personality. Up till now she'd only seen him in casual situations. And suddenly she began to realize just how he'd gotten to be the president of his own company in so short a time. Everything about him spoke of competence and authority as he faced this restive crowd. This was someone who knew how to handle himself in any situation.

Suddenly Rowan realized her mind had been wandering. She was paying more attention to the man she loved than to what was going on. Gripping her pen more tightly, she concentrated on the next question from the floor. It came from a local television newswoman named Vera Caldwell whom Rowan had run into several times on the Washington news circuit.

"Tell me, Mr. Turner," the brittle redhead was saying, "are you spouting all these statistics to obscure the real issue? The real question is, why did you run out on the Senate investigating committee?"

Brian gave the aggressive reporter a controlled smile that did not reach his eyes. "I believe I've already answered that question. There was no way I could address the committee adequately until I had all the facts myself. As soon as our investigators uncovered the real culprit I returned to Washington at once."

Ms. Caldwell was about to press the point when a strident voice to her right interrupted. "And just where were you hiding out all that time? You've never answered that question."

Brian faced his interrogator squarely. "I'm afraid I'll have to pass on that. There are other people involved."

"Does that mean you weren't alone?" an avid voice demanded.

For the first time that afternoon Brian hesitated before answering, and Rowan held her breath. "Essentially I was alone," he replied in a tight voice.

Rowan felt her heart skip a beat. What did he mean by that? Was he saying their time together meant nothing? Some of the other reporters were puzzled by this remark too and raised their hands to ask for clarification. But Brian ignored them.

"I'm afraid that's it, folks. I've said all I have to say on this issue. If you want to know anything more about our computer chips, you can direct your questions to the PR department at Turner Electronics."

A group of diehards ignored his words and tried to gather around him. Rowan recognized the tactic. It happened at many press conferences and could keep a VIP long after he'd called a halt to the formal proceedings. But Brian was clearly up to the challenge. Despite the reporters at his heels, he made his way firmly down the aisle and toward the door.

As she saw him progressing toward the exit Rowan realized that she couldn't let him get away without speaking to him. And if this was the only way she could get close to him, then so be it.

Standing up quickly, she hurried down the aisle across from the one Brian had chosen. It was clear enough that she was able to reach the door before he did. Her heart was pounding as she took up a station where a confrontation would be unavoidable. He had outdistanced most of the reporters trailing him, and as his brisk stride brought him within her range she felt her stomach knot with nervous trepidation. There was no way she could avoid meeting him face to face now. And when she saw the coldly scornful expression on his rigid features, she wished she could melt into the wall that was supporting her trembling backbone.

Brian stopped directly in front of her and looked her up and down with icy disdain. His dark eyes, which had grazed her body so warmly, were now like frozen pools of night. "I see Bill Emory has run out of original ways to plague me and is taking the more conventional route," he bit out, in a rasping whisper directed at her ears only. Bringing his face close to hers, he added, "You can tell him for me, I have no intention of giving any of his minions an exclusive interview—even if they're willing to sleep with me to get it." With that he turned on his heels and strode off.

Rowan sagged back against the mahogany paneling. She felt as though she'd just been hit in the chest by a wrecking ball. Acid tears burned the corners of her eyes. She had been a fool to come here today, to think that a face-to-face confrontation would make any difference to Brian. What was she going to do now?

CHAPTER TWELVE

Drawing on some well of reserve emotional energy she hadn't even known existed, Rowan managed to get back to the office and sit down at her typewriter. Bill would want the report of Brian's press conference immediately, she told herself woodenly as she put her mind on automatic pilot and forced herself to hammer out a summary of the main points of the meeting.

But after two sheets of paper had been filled with neat lines of type, she folded her hands over the top of the machine and rested her forehead on them. She had come back to the office in shock. But that initial protective reaction had worn off. Images of the last brief scene with Brian were beginning to sear through her consciousness. There could be absolutely no doubt now what he thought about her. Before the press conference she had been clinging to tattered shreds of hope that seeing her again would change Brian's mind. But it obviously hadn't. It had only hardened his resolve to cut her out of his life. With sudden clarity she realized she would have to come to terms with that. But how?

Thinking back, it seemed like another Rowan who had accepted the Brian Turner assignment with only thoughts of furthering her career in mind. She'd always been ambitious and competitive. And Brian was right—a lot of it had to do with her brothers and their constant challenges. But Brian had taught her there was more to life than getting ahead in a man's world. He had opened up the softness and vulnerability in her personality like a pirate uncovering buried treasure. With him she gloried in her femininity. And how could her life be complete without him now?

Somehow the things that had seemed so important before no longer held the same allure. Her work had lost its meaning. And what was more, with her new vulnerability she wondered if she were even cut out for this kind of job.

But what were the alternatives? she asked herself bleakly. What did she have left but to work herself into oblivion?

Just then Wally poked his head around the corner. He had obviously been up to something that had pleased him. His round face was flushed—and plastered with a self-satisfied smirk. Energetically rapping a little tune with his knuckles against the doorjamb, he made Rowan's head jerk up from her folded arms.

"Catching a little shut-eye on the job?" he chortled. And without waiting for an answer, he bounced jovially into the room. "Wait till I tell you about the little coup I pulled off this afternoon," he crowed. "Old Wally is really on his toes today. You're looking at the only reporter who has the inside dope on those secretaries who've been making a little cash on the side—or rather on their backs—in the hallowed halls of power."

The news might have interested Rowan a few weeks ago. But now she could only give him a dull-eyed stare.

"Say, what's wrong with you?" Wally asked. "You look like something that's just escaped from Dracula's Castle. Even your hair looks washed out, and that's some trick."

"Thanks. Your flattery might have made my day, except that it's already been made."

Wally cocked his head and narrowed his round brown eyes. In the fluorescent light his freckles stood out like miniature pennies. "I bet I know what's got you down," he announced gleefully.

Rowan glared at him and locked her jaws together. The last thing she needed was one of Wally's penetrating insights. As usual, however, the incorrigible boy sleuth was oblivious to anyone's emotions but his own.

"It's your well-heeled lover boy, isn't it? He's given you the old heave-ho. Well, don't let it get you down, Row old girl. Easy come, easy go—that's my—"

The end of his sentence was interrupted by a shower of paper clips. Rowan had picked up the box from her desk and thrown it at his head.

"Hey, what is it about the guys in the office that brings out the pitcher in you?" Wally asked, brushing a residue of the little metal shapes from his open collar and giving her an injured look.

"You insensitive clod," Rowan grated. "You wouldn't understand if I drew you a blueprint. You don't even comprehend basic human emotions."

Wally looked genuinely hurt. "What do you mean? I'm a pussycat! Besides, how was I supposed to know you were taking Turner's rejection so hard?"

He pulled up another desk chair and plopped himself down on it, facing Rowan. "Now, why don't you start from the beginning and tell old Uncle Wally all about it?"

Rowan averted her face and snorted. "You're the last person I'd talk to about this. A lot of it is your fault."

She realized she was making him the scapegoat, but at the moment her emotions stood in the way of her judgment, and it surprised her when he agreed with her unfair accusation.

"You're right, I am," he conceded in a chastened tone, "but you're responsible too. You're the one who sent us the message."

Rowan's head drooped. All her anger seemed to leak away. "Yes," she admitted in a small voice. "I did send the message, and if there was any way I could take that back, I'd walk through hell to do it."

Wally tipped his chair back, started to put his feet up

on her desk, and then changed his mind. "You really have it bad, don't you, baby?"

Rowan was still too distraught to take umbrage at the annoying endearment. "Yes. I'm in love with him." It was the first time she had said the words aloud, and it seemed ironic that she should be saying them to Wally.

"Rowan, you're a dynamite girl. You could have any man you wanted. That guy's not worth all the misery you're putting yourself through."

Though part of her brain registered the compliment with surprise, she shot him an impatient look. "Yes, he *is* worth it. He's everything I've ever wanted in a man. Brian has real principles, and he's kind, sensitive, and loyal to his friends."

"Add thrifty, reverent, and clean, and you're describing a regular Boy Scout," Wally chimed in with disgust. "But," he added quickly, with a wicked grin, "if he's passing you up he's also stupid, shortsighted, and vindictive. If, knowing that, you still want the guy, I'd say it's up to you to help him overcome his weaknesses."

Rowan frowned. "And just what do you mean by that cryptic little remark?"

"I mean," Wally explained with an air of exaggerated patience, "don't let him get away with it. Go after him. You're supposed to be smart and ambitious. Well, people who are smart and ambitious don't sit around crying about their troubles. They make the right things happen for them."

"I've already—" Rowan tried to inject. But an ant might as well have tried to stop a bulldozer rolling downhill. Wally was on one of his favorite topics and refused to be interrupted.

"Why do you think I'm the top investigative reporter in this hick town? I haven't got where I am by sitting around on my thumbs and crying into my typewriter."

Rowan blushed, remembering the bereft little waif she'd

169

been when he'd walked in. But Wally was too absorbed in self-congratulation to notice her embarrassment.

"Do you remember the time the Indian ambassador was scheduled to speak at the Cosmos Club? He wasn't giving interviews, but old Wally bribed a waiter to disappear so I could serve the ambassador his dinner. It was my first big Washington story, and I got it by using the old brainola." He tapped his head significantly. "And that was only the beginning. There was the time I played psycho to expose conditions at St. Anne's."

That shouldn't have been too much of a strain, Rowan thought privately as she listened to the complacent flow of Wally's words.

"And you were here when I did my Spiderman bit and got into the Myapollah's quarters suspended from a five-hundred-foot cable. Damn near broke my leg," he added, rubbing the threatened limb thoughtfully.

Rowan did remember this occasion. It had made front page headlines all over the world and provided her with hours of secret amusement contemplating Wally's rotund form descending on the notorious political leader from a helicopter. But he was right, she had to concede. Obnoxious though he was, he did have a way of making things go his way. As her mind turned over the implications of this Wally rambled on, telling story after story of his exploits. Most of them held little interest for her. She'd heard them dozens of times. But one did make her prick up her ears. It was the story she'd told Brian about how Wally had gotten into Natalie Wood's hotel room for an interview by posing as a maid. Picturing Wally in a dress and frilly apron made Rowan smile, despite herself, but it also gave her an idea.

Wally looked up and caught her changed expression. "Well, I can see I've really cheered you up and given you something to chew on," he said complacently.

"Yes, you have," Rowan agreed. "Of course, I could

never be quite the marvel you are, but you've got me thinking, Wally, and I have to thank you for that."

"Just remember, Rowan," he said, getting up and sauntering toward the door without bothering to push in his chair, "it's not only good ideas that count, it's the details too. Once you have a plan, you've got to check everything out and follow through. Before I dropped in on the Myapollah, I did my homework. I found out how superstitious the guy was and picked a day when his horoscope advised nonviolence."

Considerably cheered now, Rowan laughed out loud and gave him the thumbs-up sign. But after he'd made a triumphant exit, her expression once more became thoughtful and a trifle somber. She was going to make one more try at changing Brian's mind. But she couldn't even guess how it would turn out.

For the next three days Rowan used most of her spare time researching the inner workings of the Wardman Park. Using the excuse that she was a freelance writer doing an article on grand old hotels of the east coast, she learned all about the operations of their restaurant, maid service, and mail delivery. And on the pretext of learning about some of their distinguished guests, she even managed to get a good idea of Brian's habits.

When in Washington, he was usually home Saturday mornings, and although the maid was not scheduled to stop in that day this week, she did occasionally change the linen on a Saturday. She also discovered that he would be leaving for New Hampshire soon and had just shipped the antiques she'd seen in his apartment up there the day before. This information was all it took to put the wild scheme Rowan had been concocting into its final form. She knew she had to act quickly now, before Brian left the city.

Am I really crazy enough to do this? she asked herself Friday evening, staring at her pale, set image in the bathroom mirror. *The answer is yes,* she told herself grimly, taking the lid off of the round box containing the blond wig she'd purchased that afternoon at a nearby department store. When she'd tucked her red curls under the smooth, silvery pageboy, she was amazed by the transformation. She really did look like a different person. And when she'd donned the gray and white maid's uniform she'd picked up at a specialty shop and put on a pair of windowpane glasses with thick black frames, her disguise was complete. Wally would be proud of me, she thought. But what would Brian's reaction be? That was the big question.

The next morning, a uniformed, bewigged Rowan stood in front of the door to Brian's apartment. Cradled in her arms was a two-foot-high stack of neatly folded white towels which hid her face from view—and also concealed some of the special "equipment" she'd brought along.

Well, it's now or never, she told herself, taking a deep breath before raising her hand to rap smartly on the wide mahogany door. Her heart hammered in her chest as she waited for something to happen. Nothing did happen, however, until she had repeated her attack on the door three times. Her knuckles were beginning to smart when she heard an irritable male voice shout "Who is it?"

"Maid service," she managed in a quavery tone that she tried to pitch higher than her normal voice.

"Go away, I'm busy" came the inhospitable reply.

Rowan scowled over the top of her stack of terry cloth. It was just like him to be so uncooperative, she mused. Well, she hadn't gone to all this trouble to be sent away now. She knocked again, and then suddenly wondered if he had a woman in there. The thought made her want to slink away instantly. But it was too late for that. The door was thrown open and a disheveled Brian stood glowering down at her. Hastily Rowan shifted the towels so that they covered everything but her eyebrows. The glasses she was wearing had slipped uncomfortably down her nose, but she was able to push them back with the edge of a folded towel.

"What is it?" Brian snapped. "I told you I was busy."

It was obviously true. He looked disgruntled, as though he'd been making little headway with a frustrating project. Wearing blue jeans and a rumpled shirt, he was holding a small screwdriver in his right hand. A lock of thick, dark hair hung down over his forehead, curtaining one eyebrow. Rowan resisted the impulse to drop her towels and reach out to brush it back.

"I'm sorry, sir," she stammered hoarsely, trying to disguise her voice, "but I'm new here and I have to do your room before I can go home today." The excuse sounded feeble even to her own ears. But Brian seemed too preoccupied to listen closely.

"Oh, all right," he muttered. "But stay out of the dining room. I'm working in there."

"Certainly, sir," she agreed, brushing quickly past as he stood aside and then closed the door behind her. On the way to the bedroom she caught a glimpse of the dining room. One of the game machines she had seen on her first visit here had been completely dismantled and was lying on the floor in what looked like little heaps of junk. But on a hasty second inspection Rowan could see that someone had methodically arranged the piles.

Ignoring the "maid," Brian went immediately back to his work, a deep frown on his handsome face as he picked up a circuit board and a voltage meter. Now that he was no longer dressed in the impressive business suit he'd worn at the press conference, she could see that he looked paler and thinner than he had on the island. The strong lines of his face were more deeply etched and the planes of his cheekbones were prominent. But though Rowan longed to reach out to him, this was not the moment. If she revealed herself now, he might misinterpret her motives. For her plan to work, it was imperative that she get past him undetected and out of the way as soon as possible.

Once through the bedroom door, she closed it behind her, dropped her pile of towels on the floor, and then slumped against the wooden barrier with a sigh of relief. *You've got to get busy,* she told herself. But her heart was jumping around in her chest at such a rate that it was several minutes before she was collected enough to think about her next move. When she did, her first impulse was to lock the door. But she could hear Brian outside cursing under his breath as he struggled with the pile of circuitry on the dining room floor. If she could hear him, he might hear the lock snick. And she couldn't take a chance on that. So she'd have to work quickly.

First she pulled off her glasses and tossed them on the bureau. Next she lifted the mass of artificial blond waves covering her red hair and stuffed the wig into a nearby dresser drawer. It took only a moment to fluff out her own thick curls. The next five minutes were occupied with makeup. She had worn only a dash of lipstick with her disguise. But now she went to a great deal of trouble to highlight her eyes with liner and shadow, emphasize her high cheekbones with blush, and smooth on a luscious coat of deep pink lip gloss. As a final touch she dabbed her pulse points liberally with Seduction, a perfume she'd bought on impulse the day before. Its sexy name was more than appropriate for what she had in mind for Mr. Brian Turner.

Glancing down at the pile of towels strewn in front of the door, Rowan grinned. Hidden in their snowy midst was a sheer black lace nightgown calculated to weaken the resolve of a monk sworn to celibacy.

Lifting it out with one hand, she glanced quickly at the closed bedroom door. What if Brian surprised her in the act of putting it on? Well, she'd just have to take a chance on that, she thought, swiftly unbuttoning the front of her uniform. In the interest of a quick change she'd worn nothing underneath. So it was only a matter of moments before she was sliding the silky black material of the gown over her head, pulling it down over her breasts, and letting it fall gracefully around the neat curves of her hips. Pulling off her shoes, she kicked them under the bed. And soon her uniform and the pile of towels followed.

For a moment she fought to suppress a giggle. What would the real maid think if she found these? Probably that her predecessor had been dragged off by white slavers to some exotic locale in South America. And if that mythical predecessor had ever dressed in an outfit like this, Rowan thought, gazing in the mirror at her transformed image, she would have deserved her fate.

The black gown was cut square across the neck. But the demure neckline only added to the seductive effect, because the bodice was inset with an almost transparent V of black lace that came to a point just above her navel. It revealed everything but the tips of her breasts and a great deal of neighboring flesh.

The effect of the slinkily inviting gown with her fiery curls and creamy skin was spectacular. Rowan's courage almost failed her as she stared at her temptress image. What would Brian's reaction be? *Well,* she told herself grimly, turning away from the mirror and looking speculatively at the bed, *if he throws me out in this getup, then I'll really know it's all over between us.*

Head held high, Rowan stepped toward Brian's king-size bed with its brown velvet spread. Suddenly timid, she drew back the coverlet slowly and spent more time than was necessary folding it toward the foot of the bed. With a tentative hand, she reached out and touched one brown and white striped pillowcase. She could see the slight indentation of Brian's head. But the other pillow, she noted, was untouched. So he hadn't entertained a guest in his bed—last night at least. This knowledge gave her courage.

Slipping onto the yellow velour blanket, she lay down on the bed with her head where Brian's had been and sighed with relief. He could come in now, and she would be ready. But though she waited stiffly for the next fifteen minutes, he did not come in. She could still hear him rustling around outside, but he made no move toward his bedroom.

Bored and beginning to feel uncomfortable in the stiff position she'd assumed, Rowan began to shift on the bed. Recalling sexy calendar girls she'd seen, she began to try out some seductive poses. Placing her hand behind her head and thrusting her breasts forward, she pretended she was posing a la Marilyn Monroe or Bo Derek.

But she soon began to feel silly. Why wasn't Brian coming in to see what the maid was up to? Had he forgotten about her altogether? And what was more, why did he keep his apartment so cold? When she was planning this escapade, she hadn't counted on lying here freezing. Well, he had to come to bed sometime, she told herself. *And let's hope,* she added with grim humor, *that when he finally decides to head for the bedroom, he's alone.*

Rowan sighed and closed her eyes. The wait had made some of her tense excitement drain away. She'd been keyed up for days now and had spent a restless night going over and over the details of her plan. In her overheated imagination she had played out this scene countless times. But in none of those fantasy scenarios had she been forced to wait so long for Brian to appear. She closed her eyes tighter, forcing her mind to drift. An attack of nerves at this stage would do no good whatsoever.

Rowan's attempt to relax was more successful than she realized. As her mind drifted her body's exhaustion took over. Gradually, unaware of what was happening, she slipped into a deep sleep. And as she slept she pulled her knees up and curled into a ball.

Out in the dining room Brian threw down the circuit board he had been spinning between his thumbs and held up a chip to the light. The gray discoloration on one side told him the miniaturized piece of circuitry had burned out. And he didn't have a replacement. Why hadn't he thought of this possibility earlier? His afternoon taking this damn game apart and testing circuit boards had been a complete waste of time. But lately everything seemed that way, he thought with disgust. Ever since he'd discovered how little he really meant to Rowan, he'd been walking under a black cloud. Oh, sure, the diverted computer chip thing had been cleared up. But somehow that vindication hadn't made him feel much better at all. With a bitter laugh at his own expense, he recalled his brave facade for the benefit of the press. Cleve had assured him that it was a virtuoso performance. But the truth was that he'd simply responded during the question-and-answer session like a programmed robot. The only person he'd really been seeing in that room full of reporters was Rowan Strickland. Her treacherous image had been haunting his days and nights since the island. And it had taken all his strength of will to keep from pulling her into his arms when he'd encountered her at the door to the meeting room. It was only the knowledge that she was just playing another one of her devious little games that had kept him from making a fool of himself all over again.

Grimacing, Brian dropped to one knee and began to sort through some of the hardware littering the floor. He supposed he'd better start putting the machine back together now and the Lord knew how long that would take. Probably the rest of the afternoon. It would be dinnertime before he'd get this mess cleared up. But what difference did that make? He didn't have much appetite anyway. But, on second thought—why bother? Why not just ship this mess back to Turner Electronics and let someone who was paid to troubleshoot machines deal with it? Nobody would dare ask the president of the company how a machine he'd requisitioned for display purposes had gotten into this shape.

For a moment he considered dumping the whole mess into a plastic garbage bag. But the sharp points on the tiny chips might well tear through. What he needed was a canvas bag. And then he remembered the duffel he'd brought back from Larry's island. It was still at the bottom of his bedroom closet where he'd tossed it and then done his best to forget about that ill-fated trip.

Rising to his feet again, he strode in the direction of the bedroom. It was only then that he remembered the maid. Had she left? He'd been so preoccupied that he hadn't even noticed. He had already dismissed her from his mind when his hand found the knob and twisted it open. But when he stepped into the room, everything else that he'd been thinking of disappeared from his head as well.

Brian's dark eyes dilated as he stared fixedly at the broad bed in the center of the room. There, curled up in its center like a sleeping waif, was the woman who had occupied most of his waking thoughts for the past weeks. Brian's gaze traveled slowly from her bright hair to her closed eyelids. Her long, dark lashes swept the soft line of her cheek, and her pink lips were moistly parted. As Brian stood transfixed, she stirred in her sleep. He watched her lithe body uncoil, and he had to suppress a gasp as his riveted gaze encountered the transparent lace at the front of her gown. It revealed tantalizing glimpses of the swelling white mounds of her breasts. And he vividly remembered the feel of them as they had filled his hands and then pleased his lips and tongue.

Brian's breath become ragged, and there was a hard red flush along his cheekbones as his eyes swept lower. In her unconscious movements the filmy black excuse of a gown had ridden up, revealing the white flesh of Rowan's naked thighs. What was she doing here? he asked himself. This had to be some new trick. But at this moment it didn't matter. He was aching and burning for her. And she made a picture at once so vulnerable and so exciting that he could no longer continue standing motionless in the doorway. He had watched her in her sleep before, and it had always affected him powerfully. But this time the effect on him was instantaneous. He had to do something. And

178

what he wanted to do was to gather her into his arms and make love to her a thousand and one different ways all at once.

It was the feel of warm, insistent hands on her cool shoulders that awakened Rowan. The lids shielding her drowsy blue eyes lifted, and she stared up in confusion at the hard, dark face above her. Their gazes locked for a long moment. And though Brian said nothing, mere words seemed superfluous. Eagerly her naked arms reached up to encircle his strong neck and draw him close.

"Rowan," he groaned. And that was the only word spoken between them for the next few minutes. His fevered lips devoured her mouth, her cheeks, her eyelids, her neck, and the hollow of her throat where a frenzied pulse had sprung to life. Brian was like a starving man who had suddenly been offered a sumptuous feast. He couldn't get enough of her. And she in turn was just as hungry for him. Her urgent need for this man rose to meet his. She had been dreaming of Brian's touch, of his lips and hands on her flesh.

Quickly he reached for the loose neckline of her revealing gown and slipped the filmy garment down over her shoulder so that her white breasts were bared to his hot gaze, and then to his hands and lips as he lost himself in their sweet softness.

"Oh, Brian," she cried, her body twisting with unfulfilled desire while his tongue turned her nipples to throbbing nuggets of sensation.

His hands left her body only long enough to unsnap his jeans and impatiently wriggle free. In a moment they had been kicked heedlessly to the floor. It was Rowan who pulled his shirt off while he snaked the filmy nightgown down over her hips.

At last she had access to his body. Her silky-smooth legs twined eagerly with his hair-roughened ones. And her fingers joyfully kneaded the muscles of his back and shoulders. It was impossible for her to lie still. Her body wanted to move against him, to feel the friction of flesh against flesh—to surround and envelop him with her love.

"Rowan, you're driving me crazy," he gasped. He levered his lean body up above hers so that his head could move down to drop fiery kisses on the flat plane of her stomach and the softness of her thighs and hips. Rowan moaned and her fingers unconsciously twined themselves in the virile thickness of his dark hair. Her thighs parted so that his questing tongue could claim the heart of her wanting. A shiver of delight convulsed her whole body. It had been so long since she had gloried in his intimate touch.

As his body slid up so that his lips could meet hers passionately again, she reached down to bestow on him the same kind of pleasure he had given her.

If Brian's need for her had been urgent before, it was now overwhelming.

"I can't wait any longer," he muttered, his voice thick with emotion.

"You don't have to," Rowan whispered back, her own voice a ragged plea.

She felt the thrust of his male power between her legs then. And eagerly her own hips rose up to complete their embrace. The climb to the heights of ecstasy was swift for both of them. For they had each secretly focused on this moment in their imaginations. As Rowan felt a deep shudder of release pass through Brian's body she was overwhelmed by her own all-engulfing climax. The joy of it was almost too much to bear. Tears of gladness filled her eyes, and she clung to Brian as though anchoring herself against the force of a hurricane.

She wanted to go on clinging to him, to hold him close to her forever. But almost as soon as his passion had spent itself, the weight of his body left her. Her eyes snapped open, and she saw him sit up, his back squarely to her and his feet firmly on the floor.

Now that his physical need had been met, she realized,

he no longer wanted the sustaining closeness that she craved.

So their lovemaking hadn't meant the same thing to him as it had to her, she thought brokenly. It had just been a temptation he couldn't resist, not the soul-shattering experience that had brought tears to her eyes.

The thought of losing him now was unbearable. But if that was what must be, then she must store up the memory of these final moments with the man she loved. Involuntarily her hand reached out, and her fingertips brushed the warm skin of his back, memorizing the feel of his flesh.

"Don't," he commanded sharply.

The harsh syllable pierced her heart as if it had been a dagger. Biting her lip, she fought for control. Brian obviously did not want or need her love. But at least she must hold on to what dignity she had left. It was a losing battle. Although she fought desperately for control, silent tears began to leak out between her now tightly closed eyelids and trail down her cheeks.

Please, she thought. *Brian, don't turn around. Just get up off the bed and leave before you see me like this.* Despite her valiant struggle not to give her misery away, a muffled sob escaped her throat. And she felt Brian's weight shift slightly.

"Another of your tricks?" he rasped. "Are you trying to tear my guts out?"

Rowan opened her eyes. They were so wet with tears now that she saw him only as a blur. Brian had turned so that he was facing her on the bed, his face a mask of dark emotion. She struggled to answer his cruel question. But her voice was no longer under her control. Yet she had to communicate with him somehow. Pushing herself into a sitting position, she threw herself forward against his chest, her arms sliding around his neck to hold him fast. She felt the stiffness of his body, as though she were clinging to a living statue. And as her heart knew even deeper despair her tears began to flow more heavily.

It was then that the miracle happened. Slowly the stiffness went out of Brian's form. She felt his arms come up to stroke the soft flesh of her back and shoulders. And then his head bent and his lips tasted the saltiness of her tears.

"Rowan, don't do this to me," he pleaded. "I can't stand it. I love you too much to see you this way."

In wonder she raised her own face. He loved her! He had said he loved her!

The words made more tears flow, this time tears of joy, not sorrow. But she must speak now, she must. "Brian," she choked out between sobs. "Oh, Brian. I—I love you so very much. The thought of losing you hurt like—" The effort became too much again, and she simply clung to him, trying to bring her emotions under control.

He lay down on the bed then, pulling her with him so that he could soothe and rock her gently in his arms until the storm gradually subsided. It was as though she had come into a calm, safe harbor after a perilous journey.

Rowan longed to stay this way forever, warm and protected in his embrace. And yet there were things that must be said.

"Brian?" she whispered.

"Um?"

She wanted to bury her face against his chest now. But she knew that she must not hide if he were to know she was speaking the truth. Raising her head, she searched the ebony darkness of his eyes and then began to speak quickly before she lost her nerve. "Brian, I would have given anything not to have made that radio call. The morning afterwards I was in agony. That's why I told you our lovemaking had been a mistake. I was so ashamed of myself. And then I was afraid you would hate me. But I swear, I was on my way back to the cabin to tell you what I'd done when Wally and Paul showed up. After Paul hit you over the head, I tried to stay with you. They had to carry me off kicking and screaming then."

Anxiously she watched Brian's expression. But it remained calm as he reached out to stroke her cheek. For a long moment he did not speak. And she held her breath, wondering what his reaction would be.

"Rowan," he said at last. "You've got more guts than I have. I've been blaming you for what you did to me. But I've finally realized that it was as much my fault as yours. If I had just trusted you, opened up, and told you the whole story you never would have made that call."

"Oh, no, Brian, don't blame yourself," Rowan protested. But he silenced her with a gentle kiss before beginning to speak again. "And what you've just said has brought back a memory that I must have repressed. I was coming to as Wally and Paul carried you away. You were cursing like a sailor." He grinned. And Rowan blushed. "Quite a vocabulary as I remember it now, my girl."

Rowan gave in to the impulse now to hide her face. She felt Brian's lips on her hair and snuggled closer to him.

"There are things I have to tell you too," he whispered hoarsely, "things that have been keeping me awake at night."

The serious tone of his voice made her raise her head again and search his face anxiously.

"I wasn't acting very responsibly back there on the island," he explained. "I could have gotten you pregnant, you know."

Rowan felt her cheeks grow hot. "Well, it takes two to do that," she pointed out. "Brian, I thought about that too. And, of course, out there in the middle of nowhere I wasn't prepared. But I just couldn't stop myself. I wanted you too much."

"Yes, love, I know." He smiled at her tenderly and ran his hand delicately along the line of her cheekbone. "When I got back to Washington, I kept telling myself I never wanted to see you again. But at the same time I kept having this fantasy that you might be pregnant. Part of me kept hoping that you were, so I'd have to marry you."

His words brought a strong tide of emotion sweeping over Rowan. "Part of me wanted to be pregnant too," she admitted in a small voice. "I thought if I was never going to see you again, at least I'd have that. And then when I found out that I wasn't, I told myself it was for the best. . . ." she let the words trail off.

Brian tightened his strong arms around her slender body and gathered her closer against the broad wall of his chest. For a little while neither of them spoke. And then Rowan heard him chuckle.

"What's so funny?" she asked.

"I was just thinking, I've gone and put you in jeopardy again. So now you're going to have to marry me." For a moment he looked quite pleased with himself. And then his expression became worried. "Uh, that didn't come out quite the way I meant it. I don't mean that I want to marry you just because I might have gotten you pregnant. I mean I want to marry you because I love you and I want to share my life with you. You will marry me, won't you?"

"Yes. Because I love you and want to share my life with you and have your children," Rowan told him, her voice ringing with deep conviction.

Tenderly his lips sought hers then. But when she turned her face up so that her mouth could fuse with his, she felt his passion and her own rise anew.

And yet this time they both understood that there need be no hurry, that they had all the time in the world to please and entice each other.

Brian kissed the pulse point at her neck and drew in his breath appreciatively. "Umm, you smell so good. What is that perfume you're wearing?"

Rowan felt another flush spread across her cheeks. "Seduction," she whispered.

"Well, it seems to have worked," he noted with a grin, before nuzzling behind the ear.

Then he grew more serious, his dark eyes looking deeply into her blue ones. At first, each of them studied the other's face, seeing something new and joyous. There had been passion between them before. But now there was something more—the awareness of total commitment.

Languidly Rowan began to move her head so that her lips slid back and forth against Brian's—sensitive flesh against flesh. "I love you so much," she whispered, feeling the vibration of her words against his mouth and the mingling of her breath with his.

She felt his hands delicately trace the line of her eyebrows, her jaw, the outer shell of her ear.

"I love you," he repeated, using the words as a caress in the same way she had. And then he began to move his head in a new rhythm, gently capturing first her upper lip and then the lower one between his lips and teeth. The taste of him was intoxicating to her, more so than fine wine could ever be.

"Full of tricks, aren't you?" Rowan murmured with delight.

"Oh, yes." His fingers twined in the fiery curls around her face. "And what else would feel good?" his deep voice asked now, the very question making her glow with anticipation.

In answer she reached for his hands, first turning them up so that she could drop little kisses in the palms. Then she cupped them against her breasts. Sighing with pleasure, she leaned back as he began to stroke and fondle her.

She searched his face, seeing that he took as much gratification from the caresses as she did. And then she lowered her eyes to watch the way he touched her, marveling at the way the sight of his hands on her breasts intensified the sensuality of the caress.

He smiled broadly as he saw her watching him. "Tell me what feels best," he murmured, stroking his thumbs across her hardened nipples, which strained with pleasure against the teasing assault. "Is it this?" he questioned. "Or is it this?" he tried again, taking the rosy-pink points of pleasure between his thumbs and forefingers to gently squeeze and vibrate them. Rowan moaned voluptuously. And Brian's smile of self-satisfaction widened. "That must be it," he answered his own question.

"You devil," Rowan muttered. "Two can play at that kind of game you know."

She saw the glint in his dark eyes. "And what exactly do you have in mind?" he challenged.

"Just lie down and find out."

Obediently he stretched out on his back, crossing his arms behind his head. For a moment Rowan's eyes locked with his. And then, with slow deliberation, she turned away from his face.

"Now tell me what feels best," she murmured silkily, beginning to stroke the most sensitive part of his fully aroused body. "Is it this?" she questioned, moving her hand in a way she hoped was pleasing. "Or is it this?" she asked, replacing her fingers with her lips and tongue.

She was rewarded by Brian's groan of pleasure. It was a glorious feeling, knowing that she could make him respond with such fervor.

"You little witch," he gasped. "Don't you know that you're playing with fire?"

Rowan lifted her head and turned innocent blue eyes toward his dark, smoldering ones.

With strong arms he pulled her toward him and rolled her on her back so that her face was on a level with his again. They were both grinning broadly now, their passion mingled with a sense of fun.

"Now, listen," Brian protested. "I was trying to be genuinely helpful, you know."

"And so was I," Rowan countered.

"I see it's no use talking to you when you're like this," Brian growled in mock exasperation. Swiftly his lips descended to meet hers. And she opened the moist sweetness of her mouth to admit his probing tongue.

The kiss went on and on as his hands began to tangle in her hair again and then move down to stroke the sensitive skin of her neck and shoulders. Then his lips left hers to trace the same path. Rowan closed her eyes for a moment, savoring the sensuous feeling of longing he was creating in the very core of her being. When his lips reached her breasts and began an erotic little game with her pleasure-hardened nipples, she drew in her breath sharply. As she had on that first night they made love, she reached out to cradle his head against her breasts, her hands wandering luxuriously through the thick, dark forest of his hair.

It was obvious that he was remembering that first time, too. "You were beautiful in the moonlight," he whispered, his breath warm on her already superheated flesh. "But if I have my choice, I'd rather make love to you in the daytime when I can see you better."

Rowan didn't even have the decency to blush. Seeing him added so much to the intensity of the experience for her too. With an infinitely delicate touch she ran her fingers up the muscled length of his arm, down his ribs, and over his flat abdomen, following the slow progress with her eyes.

Brian captured the invading hand, to rain fiery little kisses over the fingers and palm.

Then, with a sudden urgent need, his yearning arms gathered her close. The fire in her own blood leaped up to meet his. And as he began to kiss and caress her, using the intimate knowledge he had already gained of her body to please her to the fullest, she moaned her satisfaction. Her hips began to move against his importuningly. And there could be no doubt in his mind that she was ready for him. He entered her quickly now. At once their bodies began to move together in turbulent harmony—demanding release with every ardent thrust. Wave after wave of intense feeling swept over both of them, as each whispered words of love to the other. And then both were tumbling over the edge of passion into an explosive climax. But still they

187

clung together tightly, wanting to stretch this timeless moment to its fullest.

Brian held her close to him for a long time. And for both of them there was great peace and fulfillment in the aftermath of their ardent lovemaking.

It was Rowan who finally, reluctantly, broke the comfortable silence. "Brian," she began. "I was so nervous about my maid act this morning that I couldn't get down anything but a cup of black coffee. I'm starving."

"Well, then you're about to find out one of the advantages of living in a hotel. We can send out for room service. What do you want?"

"I don't know. How about an ice cream soda?"

Brian gave her a startled look. "Are you quite sure you're not . . . ?"

"Absolutely sure. But I love ice cream sodas, and that's just the first thing that leaped into my mind."

"Well, you can have an ice cream soda for dessert, but you've had rather a strenuous afternoon. And I do think you need something a bit more substantial."

Rowan giggled. "Okay, what do I need to restore my vigor?"

Brian ran his hand suggestively up her body and across her breasts, noting that her nipples hardened at his touch. "I don't think you need anything to restore your vigor," he teased. "But you might enjoy a steak dinner. I know I would."

"You're on," Rowan told him. "If I really can get my ice cream soda for dessert—and you promise that the waiter leaves the tray in the living room. I wouldn't want anyone to see me like this."

"Why not? You look charming," Brian assured her.

After Brian had phoned down their order, Rowan slipped back into her black gown. "It's either this or the maid's uniform I kicked under the bed," she giggled.

"Actually you don't make much of a maid," Brian retorted, pulling on his jeans and shirt. "Look at this bed.

You didn't even change the sheets. You just made a total mess of them."

"Well, I did have a little help," Rowan pointed out.

"And speaking of jobs," Brian asked, changing the subject. "Are you going to keep yours after we get married?"

It was a question Rowan hadn't had much time to consider. But the answer came quite readily. "Actually I think I'm going to give up fieldwork. I wouldn't want someone else to kidnap me and carry me off to a deserted island."

Brian sighed. "That's a relief."

"Bill kept me chained to a desk for a long time," Rowan told him. "And I took you on because I was looking for some excitement. But it looks as if I'm going to be able to get all the excitement I need at home from now on. So maybe I'll go back to desk work."

Brian pulled her into his arms. "If I had my way, I'd keep you chained to the bed."

Rowan pushed away and looked up at him, her blue eyes challenging. "Now you're not going to turn out to be one of those male chauvinists, are you?" she sputtered.

"Just testing." He grinned. "I know your career is important to you. I just don't want you putting yourself in danger. Do you understand?"

Rowan nodded. "My career *is* important. And when we have kids, I'll probably freelance for a while so I can stay home with them."

"So you have it all planned," Brian marveled, pulling her into his arms again.

But a loud knock on the door interrupted their embrace. "That must be dinner," Brian informed her. "And we'd better eat. Because I have plans for the rest of the evening. You may be counting on an ice cream soda, but I'm counting on something quite different for dessert."

LOOK FOR NEXT MONTH'S
CANDLELIGHT ECSTASY ROMANCES ®

When You Want A Little More Than Romance–

Try A Candlelight Ecstasy!